FAIRY TALES
EVERY CHILD SHOULD KNOW

"THE BUTCHER OFFERED ALL THE BEANS IN HIS HAT FOR THE COW"

FAIRY TALES
EVERY CHILD SHOULD KNOW

EDITED BY
HAMILTON WRIGHT MABIE

Illustrated and Decorated by
MARY HAMILTON FRYE

Martino Publishing
Mansfield Centre, CT
2011

Martino Publishing
P.O. Box 373,
Mansfield Centre, CT 06250 USA

www.martinopublishing.com

ISBN   978-1-61427-181-9

Cover design by T. Matarazzo

Printed in the United States of America On 100% Acid-Free Paper

FAIRY TALES
EVERY CHILD SHOULD KNOW

EDITED BY
HAMILTON WRIGHT MABIE

Illustrated and Decorated by
MARY HAMILTON FRYE

GARDEN CITY PUBLISHING CO., INC.

GARDEN CITY   NEW YORK

CONTENTS

CONTENTS

ILLUSTRATIONS

The Enchanted Stag

THERE were once a brother and sister who loved each other dearly; their mother was dead, and their father had married again a woman who was most unkind and cruel to them. One day the boy took his sister's hand, and said to her, "Dear little sister, since our mother died we have not had one happy hour. Our stepmother gives us dry hard crusts for dinner and supper; she often knocks us about and threatens to kick us out of the house. Even the little dogs under the table fare better than we do, for she often throws them nice pieces to eat. Heaven pity us! Oh, if our dear mother knew! Come, let us go out into the wide world!"

3

So they went out, and wandered over fields and meadows the whole day till evening. At last they found themselves in a large forest; it began to rain, and the little sister said, "See, brother, heaven and our hearts weep together." At last, tired out with hunger and sorrow and the long journey, they crept into a hollow tree, laid themselves down, and slept till morning.

When they awoke the sun was high in the heavens and shone brightly into the hollow tree, so they left their place of shelter and wandered away in search of water.

"Oh, I am so thirsty!" said the boy. "If we could only find a brook or a stream." He stopped to listen, and said, "Stay, I think I hear a running stream." So he took his sister by the hand, and they ran together to find it.

Now the stepmother of these poor children was a wicked witch. She had seen the children go away, and, following them cautiously like a snake, had bewitched all the springs and streams in the forest. The pleasant trickling of a brook over the pebbles was heard by the children as they reached it, and the boy was just stooping to drink when the sister heard in the babbling of the brook:

"Whoever drinks of me, a tiger soon will be."

Then she cried quickly, "Stay, brother, stay! do not drink, or you will become a wild beast, and tear me to pieces."

4

THE ENCHANTED STAG

Thirsty as he was, the brother conquered his desire to drink at her words, and said, "Dear sister, I will wait till we come to a spring." So they wandered farther, but as they approached, she heard in the bubbling spring the words:

"Who drinks of me, a wolf will be."

"Brother, I pray you, do not drink of this brook; you will be changed into a wolf, and devour me."

Again the brother denied himself and promised to wait; but he said, "At the next stream I must drink, say what you will, my thirst is so great."

Not far off ran a pretty streamlet, looking clear and bright; but here also in its murmuring waters the sister heard the words:

"Who dares to drink of me,
Turned to a stag will be."

"Dear brother, do not drink," she began; but she was too late, for her brother had already knelt by the stream to drink, and as the first drop of water touched his lips he became a fawn. How the little sister wept over the enchanted brother, and the fawn wept also.

He did not run away, but stayed close to her; and at last she said, "Stand still, dear fawn; don't fear, I must take care of you, but I will never leave you." So she untied her little golden garter and fastened it around the

5

neck of the fawn; then she gathered some soft green rushes and braided them into a soft string, which she fastened to the fawn's golden collar, and then led him away into the depths of the forest.

After wandering about for some time, they at last found a little deserted hut, and the sister was overjoyed, for she thought it would form a nice shelter for them both. So she led the fawn in, and then went out alone to gather moss and dried leaves to make him a soft bed.

Every morning she went out to gather dried roots, nuts, and berries for her own food, and sweet fresh grass for the fawn, which he ate out of her hand, and the poor little animal went out with her and played about as happy as the day was long.

When evening came, and the poor sister felt tired, she would kneel down and say her prayers, and then lay her delicate head on the fawn's back, which was a soft warm pillow on which she could sleep peacefully. Had this dear brother only kept his own proper form, how happy they would have been together! After they had been alone in the forest for some time, and the little sister had grown a lovely maiden and the fawn a large stag, a numerous hunting party came to the forest, and amongst them the king of the country.

The sounding horn, the barking of the dogs, the holloa of the huntsmen, resounded through the forest

6

and were heard by the stag, who became eager to join his companions.

"Oh, dear," he said, "do let me go and see the hunt; I cannot restrain myself." And he begged so hard that at last she reluctantly consented.

"But remember," she said, "I must lock the cottage door against those huntsmen, so when you come back in the evening, and knock, I shall not admit you unless you say, 'Dear little sister, let me in.'"

He bounded off as she spoke, scarcely stopping to listen, for it was so delightful for him to breathe the fresh air and be free again.

He had not run far when the king's chief hunter caught sight of the beautiful animal and started off in chase of him; but it was no easy matter to overtake such rapid footsteps. Once, when he thought he had him safe, the fawn sprang over the bushes and disappeared.

As it was now nearly dark, he ran up to the little cottage, knocked at the door, and cried, "Dear little sister, let me in." The door was instantly opened, and oh, how glad his sister was to see him safely resting on his soft pleasant bed!

A few days after this the huntsmen were again in the forest; and when the fawn heard the holloa, he could not rest in peace, but begged his sister again to let him go.

She opened the door, and said, "I will let you go this time; but pray do not forget to say what I told you, when you return this evening."

The chief hunter very soon espied the beautiful fawn with the golden collar, pointed it out to the king, and they determined to hunt it.

They chased him with all their skill till the evening; but he was too light and nimble for them to catch, till a shot wounded him slightly in the foot, so that he was obliged to hide himself in the bushes, and, after the huntsmen were gone, limp slowly home.

One of them, however, determined to follow him at a distance, and discover where he went. What was his surprise at seeing him go up to a door and knock, and to hear him say, "Dear little sister, let me in." The door was only opened a little way, and quickly shut; but the huntsman had seen enough to make him full of wonder when he returned and described to the king what he had seen.

"We will have one more chase to-morrow," said the king, "and discover this mystery."

In the meantime the loving sister was terribly alarmed at finding the stag's foot wounded and bleeding. She quickly washed off the blood, and, after bathing the wound, placed healing herbs on it, and said, "Lie down on your bed, dear fawn, and the wound will soon heal if you rest your foot."

8

In the morning the wound was so much better that the fawn felt the foot almost as strong as ever, and so, when he again heard the holloa of the hunters, he could not rest. "Oh, dear sister, I must go once more; it will be easy for me to avoid the hunters now, and my foot feels quite well; they will not hunt me unless they see me running, and I don't mean to do that."

But his sister wept, and begged him not to go: "If they kill you, dear fawn, I shall be here alone in the forest, forsaken by the whole world."

"And I shall die of grief," he said, "if I remain here listening to the hunter's horn."

So at length his sister, with a heavy heart, set him free, and he bounded away joyfully into the forest.

As soon as the king caught sight of him, he said to the huntsmen, "Follow that stag about, but don't hurt him." So they hunted him all day, but at the approach of sunset the king said to the hunter who had followed the fawn the day before, "Come and show me the little cottage."

So they went together, and when the king saw it he sent his companion home, and went on alone so quickly that he arrived there before the fawn; and, going up to the little door, knocked and said softly, "Dear little sister, let me in."

As the door opened the king stepped in, and in great astonishment saw a maiden more beautiful than he had ever seen in his life standing before him. But how frightened she felt to see instead of her dear little fawn a noble gentleman walk in with a gold crown on his head.

However, he appeared very friendly, and after a little talk he held out his hand to her, and said, "Wilt thou go with me to my castle and be my dear wife?"

"Ah yes," replied the maiden, "I would willingly; but I cannot leave my dear fawn: he must go with me wherever I am."

"He shall remain with you as long as you live," replied the king, "and I will never ask you to forsake him."

While they were talking the fawn came bounding in, looking quite well and happy. Then his sister fastened the string of rushes to his collar, took it in her hand, and led him away from the cottage in the wood to where the king's beautiful horse waited for him.

The king placed the maiden before him on his horse and rode away to his castle, the fawn following by their side. Soon after their marriage was celebrated with great splendour, and the fawn was taken the greatest care of, and played where he pleased or roamed about the castle grounds in happiness and safety.

In the meantime the wicked stepmother, who had caused these two young people such misery, supposed that the sister had been devoured by wild beasts and

"THEY RODE AWAY TO HIS CASTLE, THE FAWN FOLLOWING BY THEIR SIDE."

that the fawn had been hunted to death. Therefore when she heard of their happiness, such envy and malice arose in her heart that she could find no rest till she had tried to destroy it.

She and her ugly daughter came to the castle when the queen had a little baby, and one of them pretended to be a nurse, and at last got the mother and child into their power.

They shut the queen up in the bath and tried to suffocate her, and the old woman put her own ugly daughter in the queen's bed that the king might not know she was away.

She would not, however, let him speak to her, but pretended that she must be kept quite quiet.

The queen escaped from the bathroom, where the wicked old woman had locked her up, but she did not go far, as she wanted to watch over her child and the little fawn.

For two nights the baby's nurse saw a figure of the queen come into the room and take up her baby and nurse it. Then she told the king, and he determined to watch himself. The old stepmother, who acted as nurse to her ugly daughter, whom she tried to make the king believe was his wife, had said that the queen was too weak to see him, and never left her room. "There cannot be two queens," said the king to himself, "so to-night I will watch in the nursery." As soon as the figure came in and took up her baby, he saw it was his real wife, and caught her in his arms, saying, "You are my own beloved wife, as beautiful as ever."

The wicked witch had thrown her into a trance, hoping she would die and that the king would then marry her daughter; but on the king speaking to her, the spell was broken. The queen told the king how cruelly she had been treated by her stepmother, and on hearing this he became very angry and had the witch and her daughter brought to justice. They were both sentenced to die—the daughter to be devoured by wild beasts and the mother to be burnt alive.

No sooner, however, was she reduced to ashes than the charm which held the queen's brother in the form of a stag was broken; he recovered his own natural shape, and appeared before them a tall, handsome young man.

After this the brother and sister lived happily and peacefully for the rest of their lives.

THE TWELVE BROTHERS

THERE were once a king and queen who had
twelve children—all boys. Now, one day the
king told his wife that if a daughter should be
born all the sons must die—that their sister alone might
inherit his kingdom and riches.

So the king had twelve coffins made, which were
filled with shavings, and in each was the little pillow
for the dead. He had them locked up in a private
room, the key of which he gave to the queen, pray-
ing her not to speak of it to any one. But the poor
mother was so unhappy that she wept for a whole
day, and looked so sad that her youngest son noticed
it.

He had the Bible name of Benjamin, and was always with his mother.

"Dear mother," he said, "why are you so sorrowful?"

"My child, I may not tell you," she replied; but the boy allowed her no rest till she unlocked the door of the private room and showed him the twelve coffins filled with shavings.

"Dearest Benjamin," she said, "these coffins are for you and your brothers; for if you should ever have a little sister you will all die and be buried in them."

She wept bitterly as she told him, but her son comforted her, and said, "Do not weep, dear mother. We will take care of ourselves, and go far away."

Then she took courage, and said, "Yes, go away with your eleven brothers, and remain in the forest; and let one climb a tree, from whence he will be able to see the tower of the castle. If I should have a son, a white flag shall be hoisted, and then you may return home; but if you see a red flag, you will know it is a girl, and then hasten away as fast as you can, and may Heaven protect you! Every night I will pray for you, that you may not suffer from the cold in winter nor the heat in summer."

Then she blessed all her sons, and they went away into the forest, while each in turn mounted a high tree daily, to watch for the flag on the tower.

14

THE TWELVE BROTHERS

Eleven days passed, and it was Benjamin's turn to watch. He saw the flag hoisted, and it was red—the signal that they must die. The brothers were angry, and said, "Shall we suffer death on account of a maiden? When we find one we will kill her, to avenge ourselves."

They went still farther into the forest, and came upon a most pleasant little cottage which was uninhabited. "We will make this our home," they said; "and Benjamin, as you are the youngest and weakest, you shall stay at home and keep house while we go out and procure food."

So they wandered about the forest, shooting hares, wild rabbits, pigeons and other birds, which they brought to Benjamin to prepare for food. In this cottage they lived for ten years happily together, so that the time passed quickly.

Their little sister was growing a great girl. She had a sweet disposition, and was very beautiful to look upon. She wore rich clothes and a golden star on her forehead.

One day, when she was about ten years old, she discovered in her mother's wardrobe twelve shirts.

"Mother," she exclaimed, "whose shirts are these? They are much too small for my father."

The queen sighed as she replied, "Dear child, these shirts belong to your twelve brothers."

"Twelve brothers!" cried the little maiden. "Where are they? I have not even heard of them."

"Heaven knows where they are," was the reply; "but they are wandering about the world somewhere." Then the queen took her little daughter to the private room in the castle and showed her the twelve coffins which had been prepared for her brothers, and related to her, with many tears, why they had left home.

"Dear mother," said the child, "do not weep. I will go and seek my brothers." So she took the twelve shirts with her and wandered away into the forest.

She walked for a whole day, and in the evening came to a cottage, stepped in, and found a young boy, who stared with astonishment at seeing a beautiful little girl dressed in rich clothing and wearing a golden star on her forehead.

At last he said, "Who are you, and what do you want?"

"I am a king's daughter," she said, "and I seek my twelve brothers, and I intend to search for them till I find them"; and she showed him their shirts.

Then Benjamin knew that she was his sister, and said, "I am your youngest brother, Benjamin." Then she wept for joy. They kissed each other with deep affection, and were for a time very happy.

At last Benjamin said, "Dear sister, we have made a vow that the first young maiden we meet should die, because through a maiden we have lost our kingly rights."

16

"I would willingly die," she said, "if by so doing I could restore my brothers to their rightful possessions."

"No, you shall not die," he replied. "Hide yourself behind this tub until our eleven brothers come home; then I will make an agreement with them."

At night the brothers returned from hunting, and the supper was ready. While they sat at table, one of them said, "Well, Benjamin, have you any news?"

"Perhaps I have," he said, "although it seems strange that I who stay at home should know more than you who have been out."

"Well, tell us your news," said one. So he said: "I will tell you if you will make one promise."

"Yes, yes!" they all cried. "What is it?"

"Well, then, promise me that the first maiden you meet with in the forest shall *not* die."

"Yes, yes!" said they all; "she shall have mercy; but tell us."

"Then," said the youngest brother, "our sister is here"; and rising, he lifted the tub, and the king's daughter came forth in her royal robes and with a golden star on her forehead, and looking so fair and delicate and beautiful that the brothers were full of joy, and kissed and embraced her with the fondest affection.

She stayed with Benjamin, and helped him in keeping the house clean and cooking the game which the others brought home. Everything was so nicely managed now and with so much order; the curtains and the quilts were beautifully white, and the dinners cooked so well that the brothers were always contented, and lived in great unity with their little sister.

There was a pretty garden around the house in which they lived, and one day, when they were all at home dining together and enjoying themselves, the maiden went out into the garden to gather them some flowers.

She had tended twelve lilies with great care, and they were now in such splendid bloom that she determined to pluck them for her brothers, to please them.

But the moment she gathered the lilies her twelve brothers were changed into twelve ravens, and flew away over the trees of the forest, while the charming house and garden vanished from her sight. Now was the poor little maiden left all alone in the wild wood, and knew not what to do; but on turning round she saw a curious old woman standing near, who said to her, "My child, what hast thou done? Why didst thou not leave those white flowers to grow on their stems? They were thy twelve brothers, and now they will always remain ravens."

"Is there no way to set them free?" asked the maiden, weeping.

"No way in the world," she replied, "but one, and that is far too difficult for thee to perform; yet it would

18

"THE BROTHERS WERE FULL OF JOY, AND EMBRACED HER WITH FONDEST AFFECTION"

break the spell and set them free. Hast thou firmness enough to remain dumb seven years, and not speak to any one or even laugh? For if ever you utter a single word or fail only once in the seven years, all you have done before will be vain, and at this one word your brothers will die."

"Yes," said the maiden, "I can do this to set my brothers free."

Then the maiden climbed into a tree, and, seating herself in the branches, began to knit.

She remained here, living on the fruit that grew on the tree, and without laughing or uttering a word.

As she sat in her tree, the king, who was hunting, had a favourite hound, who very soon discovered her, ran to the tree on which the maiden sat, sprang up to it, and barked at her violently.

The king came nearer, and saw the beautiful king's daughter with the golden star on her forehead. He was so struck with her beauty that he begged her to come down, and asked her to be his bride. She did not speak a word, but merely nodded her head. Then the king himself climbed up into the tree, and, bringing her down, seated her on his own horse and galloped away with her to his home.

The marriage was soon after celebrated with great pomp, but the bride neither spoke nor laughed.

When they had lived happily together for some

years, the king's mother, a wicked woman, began to raise evil reports about the queen, and said to the king, "It is some beggar girl you have picked up. Who can tell what wicked tricks she practises. She can't help being dumb, but why does she never laugh?—unless she has a guilty conscience?" The king at first would listen to none of these suspicions, but she urged him so long and accused the queen of such wicked conduct, that at last he condemned her to be burnt to death.

Now in the courtyard a great fire was kindled, and the king stood weeping at a window overlooking the court of the palace, for he still loved her dearly. He saw her brought forth and tied to the stake; the fire was kindled, and the flames with their forked tongues were creeping toward her, when at the last moment the seven years were past, and suddenly a rustling noise of wings was heard in the air; twelve black ravens alighted on the earth and instantly assumed their own forms— they were the brothers of the queen.

They tore down the pile and extinguished the fire, set their sister free, and embraced her tenderly. The queen, who was now able to speak, told the king why she had been dumb and had never laughed.

The delight of the king was only equalled by his anger against the wicked witch, who was brought to justice and ordered to be thrown into a vat of oil full of poisonous snakes, where she died a dreadful death.

PUSS IN BOOTS

THERE was a miller who had three sons, and when he died he divided what he possessed among them in the following manner: He gave his mill to the eldest, his ass to the second, and his cat to the youngest. Each of the brothers accordingly took what belonged to him, without the help of an attorney, who would soon have brought their little fortune to nothing in law expenses. The poor young fellow who had nothing but the cat complained that he was hardly used: "My brothers," said he, "by joining their stocks together may do well in the world, but for me, when I have eaten my cat and made a fur cap of his skin, I may soon die of hunger!" The cat,

21

who all this time sat listening just inside the door of a cupboard, now ventured to come out and addressed him as follows: "Do not thus afflict yourself, my good master. You have only to give me a bag, and get a pair of boots made for me, so that I may scamper through the dirt and the brambles, and you shall see that you are not so ill provided for as you imagine." Though the cat's master did not much depend upon these promises, yet, as he had often observed the cunning tricks puss used to catch the rats and mice, such as hanging upon his hind legs and hiding in the meal to make believe that he was dead, he did not entirely despair of his being of some use to him in his unhappy condition.

When the cat had obtained what he asked for, he gayly began to equip himself: he drew on his boots; and putting the bag about his neck, he took hold of the strings with his forepaws, and bidding his master take courage, immediately sallied forth. The first attempt Puss made was to go into a warren in which there were a great number of rabbits. He put some bran and some parsley into his bag; and then stretching himself out at full length as if he was dead, he waited for some young rabbits, who as yet knew nothing of the cunning tricks of the world, to come and get into the bag, the better to feast upon the dainties he had put into it. Scarcely had he lain down before he succeeded as well as could be wished. A giddy young rabbit crept into the bag, and the cat immediately drew the strings and killed him without mercy. Puss, proud of his prey, hastened directly to the palace, where he asked to speak to the king. On being shown into the apartment of his Majesty, he made a low bow, and said, "I have brought you, Sire, this rabbit from the warren of my lord, the marquis of Carabas, who commanded me to present it to your Majesty with the assurance of his respect." (This was the title the cat thought proper to bestow upon his master.) "Tell my lord marquis of Carabas," replied the king, "that I accept of his present with pleasure and that I am greatly obliged to him." Soon after, the cat laid himself down in the same manner in a field of corn, and had as much good fortune as before; for two fine partridges got into his bag, which he immediately killed and carried to the palace; the king received them as he had done the rabbit, and ordered his servants to give the messenger something to drink. In this manner he continued to carry presents of game to the king from my lord marquis of Carabas at least once in every week.

One day, the cat having heard that the king intended to take a ride that morning by the river's side with his daughter, who was the most beautiful princess in the world, he said to his master: "If you will but follow my advice, your fortune is made. Take off your clothes, and bathe yourself in the river, just in the

23

place I shall show you, and leave the rest to me." The marquis of Carabas did exactly as he was desired, without being able to guess at what the cat intended. While he was bathing the king passed by, and Puss directly called out as loud as he could bawl: "Help! help! My lord marquis of Carabas is in danger of being drowned!" The king, hearing the cries, put his head out at the window of his carriage to see what was the matter: when, perceiving the very cat who had brought him so many presents, he ordered his attendants to go directly to the assistance of my lord marquis of Carabas. While they were employed in taking the marquis out of the river, the cat ran to the king's carriage, and told his Majesty that while his master was bathing some thieves had run off with his clothes as they lay by the river's side; the cunning cat all the time having hid them under a large stone. The king, hearing this, commanded the officers of his wardrobe to fetch one of the handsomest suits it contained, and present it to my lord marquis of Carabas, at the same time loading him with a thousand attentions. As the fine clothes they brought him made him look like a gentleman, and set off his person, which was very comely, to the greatest advantage, the king's daughter was mightily taken with his appearance, and the marquis of Carabas had no sooner cast upon her two or three respectful glances, than she became violently in love with him.

The king insisted on his getting into the carriage and taking a ride with them. The cat, enchanted to see how well his scheme was likely to succeed, ran before to a meadow that was reaping, and said to the reapers: "Good people, if you do not tell the king, who will soon pass this way, that the meadow you are reaping belongs to my lord marquis of Carabas, you shall be chopped as small as mince meat." The king did not fail to ask the reapers to whom the meadow belonged. "To my lord marquis of Carabas," said they all at once; for the threats of the cat had terribly frighted them. "You have here a very fine piece of land, my lord marquis," said the king. "Truly, Sire," replied he, "it does not fail to bring me every year a plentiful harvest." The cat, who still went on before, now came to a field where some other labourers were making sheaves of the corn they had reaped, to whom he said as before: "Good people, if you do not tell the king, who will presently pass this way, that the corn you have reaped in this field belongs to my lord marquis of Carabas, you shall be chopped as small as mince meat." The king accordingly passed a moment after, and inquired to whom the corn he saw belonged. "To my lord marquis of Carabas," answered they very glibly; upon which the king again complimented the marquis upon his noble possessions. The cat still continued to go before, and gave the same charge to all the people he met with; so that the king was greatly astonished at the splendid fortune of my lord marquis of Carabas. Puss at length arrived at a stately castle which belonged to an Ogre, the richest ever known; for all the lands the king had passed through and admired were his. The cat took care to learn every particular about the Ogre, and what he could do, and then asked to speak with him, saying, as he entered the room in which he was, that he could not pass so near his castle without doing himself the honour to inquire after his health. The Ogre received him as civilly as an Ogre could do, and desired him to be seated. "I have been informed," said the cat, "that you have the gift of changing yourself to all sorts of animals, into a lion or an elephant for example." "It is very true," replied the Ogre somewhat sternly; "and to convince you I will directly take the form of a lion." The cat was so much terrified at finding himself so near to a lion that he sprang from him, and climbed to the roof of the house; but not without much difficulty, as his boots were not very fit to walk upon the tiles.

Some minutes after, the cat perceiving that the Ogre had quitted the form of a lion, ventured to come down from the tiles, and owned that he had been a good deal frightened. "I have been further informed," continued the cat, "but I know not how to believe it, that you have the power of taking the form of the smallest

"THE MILLER GAVE HIS CAT TO THE YOUNGEST SON"

animals also; for example of changing yourself to a rat or a mouse: I confess I should think this impossible." "Impossible! you shall see"; and at the same instant he changed himself into a mouse, and began to frisk about the room. The cat no sooner cast his eyes upon the Ogre in this form, than he sprang upon him and devoured him in an instant. In the meantime the king, admiring as he came near it, the magnificent castle of the Ogre, ordered his attendants to drive up to the gates, as he wished to take a nearer view of it. The cat, hearing the noise of the carriage on the drawbridge, immediately came out, saying: "Your Majesty is welcome to the castle of my lord marquis of Carabas." "And is this splendid castle yours also, my lord marquis of Carabas? I never saw anything more stately than the building, or more beautiful than the park and pleasure grounds around it; no doubt the castle is no less magnificent within than without: pray, my lord marquis, indulge me with a sight of it."

The marquis gave his hand to the young princess as she alighted, and followed the king who went before; they entered a spacious hall, where they found a splendid collation which the Ogre had prepared for some friends he had that day expected to visit him; but who, hearing that the king with the princess and a great gentleman of the court were within, had not dared to enter. The king was so much charmed with the amiable qualities and noble fortune of the marquis of Car-abas, and the young princess, too, had fallen so violently in love with him, that when the king had partaken of the collation, and drunk a few glasses of wine, he said to the marquis: "It will be your own fault, my lord marquis of Carabas, if you do not soon become my son-in-law." The marquis received the intelligence with a thousand respectful acknowledgments, accepted the honour conferred upon him, and married the princess that very day. The cat became a great lord, and never after ran after rats and mice but for his amusement.

JACK AND THE BEANSTALK

IN THE days of King Alfred there lived a poor woman whose cottage was situated in a remote country village, a great many miles from London. She had been a widow some years, and had an only child named Jack, whom she indulged to a fault. The consequence of her blind partiality was that Jack did not pay the least attention to anything she said, but was indolent, careless, and extravagant. His follies were not owing to a bad disposition, but that his mother had never checked him. By degrees she disposed of all she possessed—scarcely anything remained but a cow. The poor woman one day met Jack with tears in her eyes; her distress was great, and for the first time in her life she could not help reproaching him, saying, "Oh! you wicked child, by your ungrateful course of life you have at last brought me to beggary and ruin. Cruel, cruel boy! I have not money enough to purchase even a bit of bread for another day—nothing now remains to sell but my poor cow! I am sorry to part with her; it grieves me sadly, but we must not starve." For a few minutes Jack felt a degree of remorse, but it was soon over, and he began teasing his mother to let him sell the cow at the next village, so much that she at last consented. As he was going along he met a butcher, who inquired why he was driving the cow from home. Jack replied he was going to sell it. The butcher held some curious beans in his hat; they were of various colours and attracted Jack's attention. This did not pass unnoticed by the butcher, who, knowing Jack's easy temper, thought now was the time to take an advantage of it, and determined not to let slip so good an opportunity, asked what was the price of the cow, offering at the same time all the beans in his hat for her. The silly boy could not conceal the pleasure he felt at what he supposed so great an offer, the bargain was struck instantly, and the cow exchanged for a few paltry beans. Jack made the best of his way home, calling aloud to his mother before he reached home, thinking to surprise her.

When she saw the beans, and heard Jack's account,

her patience quite forsook her. She kicked the beans away in a passion—they flew in all directions—some were scattered in the garden. Not having anything to eat, they both went supperless to bed. Jack woke early in the morning, and seeing something uncommon from the window of his bedchamber, ran downstairs into the garden, where he soon discovered that some of the beans had taken root and sprung up surprisingly: the stalks were of an immense thickness, and had so entwined that they formed a ladder nearly like a chain in appearance. Looking upward, he could not discern the top, it appeared to be lost in the clouds: he tried it, found it firm, and not to be shaken. He quickly formed the resolution of endeavouring to climb up to the top in order to seek his fortune, and ran to communicate his intention to his mother, not doubting but she would be equally pleased with himself. She declared he should not go; said it would break her heart if he did—entreated and threatened—but all in vain. Jack set out, and after climbing for some hours, reached the top of the beanstalk, fatigued and quite exhausted. Looking around, he found himself in a strange country; it appeared to be a desert, quite barren, not a tree, shrub, house, or living creature to be seen; here and there were scattered fragments of stone; and at unequal distances, small heaps of earth were loosely thrown together.

Jack seated himself pensively upon a block of stone,

and thought of his mother—he reflected with sorrow upon his disobedience in climbing the beanstalk against her will; and concluded that he must die with hunger. However, he walked on, hoping to see a house where he might beg something to eat and drink; presently a handsome young woman appeared at a distance; as she approached, Jack could not help admiring how beautiful and lively she looked. She was dressed in the most elegant manner, and had a small white wand in her hand, on the top of which was a peacock of pure gold. While Jack was looking with great surprise at this charming female, she came up to him, and with a smile of the most bewitching sweetness, inquired how he came there. Jack related the circumstance of the beanstalk. She asked him if he recollected his father; he replied he did not; and added, there must be some mystery relating to him, because if he asked his mother who his father was, she always burst into tears and appeared violently agitated, nor did she recover herself for some days after; one thing, however, he could not avoid observing upon these occasions, which was that she always carefully avoided answering him, and even seemed afraid of speaking, as if there was some secret connected with his father's history which she must not disclose. The young woman replied, "I will reveal the whole story; your mother must not. But before I begin, I require a solemn promise on your part to do what I command; I am a fairy, and if you do not perform exactly what I desire, you will be destroyed." Jack was frightened at her menaces, but promised to fulfil her injunctions exactly, and the fairy thus addressed him:

"Your father was a rich man, his disposition remarkably benevolent: he was very good to the poor and constantly relieving them. He made it a rule never to let a day pass without doing good to some person. On one particular day in the week he kept open house, and invited only those who were reduced and had lived well. He always presided himself, and did all in his power to render his guests comfortable; the rich and the great were not invited. The servants were all happy and greatly attached to their master and mistress. Your father, though only a private gentleman, was as rich as a prince, and he deserved all he possessed, for he only lived to do good. Such a man was soon known and talked of. A giant lived a great many miles off: this man was altogether as wicked as your father was good; he was in his heart envious, covetous, and cruel; but he had the art of concealing these vices. He was poor, and wished to enrich himself at any rate. Hearing your father spoken of, he formed the design of becoming acquainted with him, hoping to ingratiate himself into your father's favour. He removed quickly into your neighbourhood, caused to be reported that he was a gentleman who had just lost all he possessed by an earthquake, and found it difficult to escape with his life; his wife was with him. Your father gave credit to his story, and pitied him, gave him handsome apartments in his own house, and caused him and his wife to be treated like visitors of consequence, little imagining that the giant was meditating a horrid return for all his favours.

"Things went on in this way for some time, the giant becoming daily more impatient to put his plan into execution; at last a favourable opportunity presented itself. Your father's house was at some distance from the seashore, but with a glass the coast could be seen distinctly. The giant was one day using the telescope; the wind was very high; he saw a fleet of ships in distress off the rocks; he hastened to your father, mentioned the circumstance, and eagerly requested he would send all the servants he could spare to relieve the sufferers. Every one was instantly dispatched except the porter and your nurse; the giant then joined your father in the study, and appeared to be delighted—he really was so. Your father recommended a favourite book and was handing it down; the giant took the opportunity and stabbed him; he instantly fell down dead. The giant left the body, found the porter and nurse, and presently dispatched them, being determined to have no living witnesses of his crimes. You were then only three months old; your mother had you in her arms in a re-

mote part of the house, and was ignorant of what was
going on; she went into the study, but how was she
shocked on discovering your father a corpse and wel-
tering in his blood! She was stupefied with horror and
grief, and was motionless. The giant, who was seeking
her, found her in that state, and hastened to serve her
and you as he had done her husband, but she fell at his
feet, and in a pathetic manner besought him to spare
your life and hers.

"Remorse, for a moment, seemed to touch the bar-
barian's heart: he granted your lives; but first he made
her take a most solemn oath never to inform you who
your father was or to answer any questions concerning
him, assuring her that if she did, he would certainly
discover her and put both of you to death in the most
cruel manner. Your mother took you in her arms
and fled as quickly as possible; she was scarcely gone
when the giant repented that he had suffered her to
escape. He would have pursued her instantly, but he
had to provide for his own safety, as it was necessary
he should be gone before the servants returned. Having gained your father's confidence, he knew where to
find all his treasure; he soon loaded himself and his wife,
set the house on fire in several places, and when the
servants returned the house was burned quite down to
the ground. Your poor mother, forlorn, abandoned,
and forsaken, wandered with you a great many miles

from this scene of desolation. Fear added to her haste. She settled in the cottage where you were brought up, and it was entirely owing to her fear of the giant that she never mentioned your father to you. I became your father's guardian at his birth, but fairies have laws to which they are subject as well as mortals. A short time before the giant went to your father's, I transgressed; my punishment was a suspension of power for a limited time—an unfortunate circumstance, as it totally prevented my succouring your father.

"The day on which you met the butcher, as you went to sell your mother's cow, my power was restored. It was I who secretly prompted you to take the beans in exchange for the cow. By my power, the beanstalk grew to so great a height, and formed a ladder. I need not add that I inspired you with a strong desire to ascend the ladder. The giant lives in this country; you are the person appointed to punish him for all his wickedness. You will have dangers and difficulties to encounter, but you must persevere in avenging the death of your father or you will not prosper in any of your undertakings, but will always be miserable. As to the giant's possessions, you may seize on all you can, for everything he has is yours, though now you are unjustly deprived of it. One thing I desire—do not let your mother know you are acquainted with your father's history till you see me again. Go along the direct road; you will soon see the house where your cruel enemy lives. While you do as I order you, I will protect and guard you; but, remember, if you dare disobey my commands a most dreadful punishment awaits you."

When the fairy had concluded she disappeared, leaving Jack to pursue his journey. He walked on till after sunset, when, to his great joy, he espied a large mansion. This agreeable sight revived his drooping spirits; he redoubled his speed, and soon reached it. A plain-looking woman was at the door—he accosted her, begging she would give him a morsel of bread and a night's lodging. She expressed the greatest surprise at seeing him, and said it was quite uncommon to see a human being near their house, for it was well known that her husband was a large and very powerful giant, that he would never eat anything but human flesh if he could possibly get it, and that he did not think anything of walking fifty miles to procure it, usually being out the whole day for that purpose.

This account greatly terrified Jack, but still he hoped to elude the giant, and therefore he again entreated the woman to take him in for one night only, and hide him where she thought proper. The good woman at last suffered herself to be persuaded, for she was of a compassionate and generous disposition, and took him into the house. First, they entered a fine large hall, magnificently furnished; they then passed through several spacious rooms, all in the same style of grandeur, but they appeared to be quite forsaken and desolate. A long gallery was next; it was very dark—just light enough to show that instead of a wall on one side there was a grating of iron, which parted off a dismal dungeon, from whence issued the groans of those poor victims whom the cruel giant reserved in confinement for his own voracious appetite. Poor Jack was half dead with fear, and would have given the world to have been with his mother again, for he now began to fear that he should never see her more, and gave himself up for lost; he even mistrusted the good woman, and thought she had let him into the house for no other purpose than to lock him up among the unfortunate people in the dungeon. At the farther end of the gallery there was a spacious kitchen and a very excellent fire was burning in the grate. The good woman bade Jack sit down, and gave him plenty to eat and drink. Jack, not seeing anything here to make him uncomfortable, soon forgot his fear, and was just beginning to enjoy himself when he was aroused by a loud knocking at the street door which made the whole house shake; the giant's wife ran to secure him in the oven, and then went to let her husband in. Jack heard him accost her in a voice like thunder, saying: "Wife, I smell fresh meat." "Oh! my dear," replied she, "it is nothing but the people in the dungeon." The giant appeared to believe her, and walked into the very kitchen where poor Jack was concealed, who shook, trembled, and was more terrified than he had yet been. At last the monster seated himself quietly by the fireside, whilst his wife prepared supper. By degrees Jack recovered himself sufficiently to look at the giant through a small crevice. He was quite astonished to see what an amazing quantity he devoured, and thought he never would have done eating and drinking. When supper was ended, the giant desired his wife to bring him his hen. A very beautiful hen was then brought and placed on the table before him. Jack's curiosity was very great to see what would happen; he observed that every time the giant said "Lay!" the hen laid an egg of solid gold. The giant amused himself a long time with his hen; meanwhile his wife went to bed. At length the giant fell asleep by the fireside, and snored like the roaring of a cannon.

At daybreak, Jack, finding the giant still asleep and not likely to awaken soon, crept softly out of his hiding-place, seized the hen, and ran off with her. He met with some difficulty in finding his way out of the house, but at last he reached the road with safety. He easily found the way to the beanstalk, and descended it better and quicker than he expected. His mother was overjoyed to see him; he found her crying bitterly and lamenting his hard fate, for she concluded he had come to some shocking end through his rashness. Jack was impatient to show his hen and inform his mother how valuable it was. "And now, mother," said Jack, "I have brought home that which will quickly make us rich; and I hope to make you some amends for the affliction I have caused you through my idleness, extravagance, and folly." The hen produced as many golden eggs as they desired; they sold them, and in a little time became possessed of as much riches as they wanted. For some months Jack and his mother lived very happily together; but he, being very desirous of travelling, recollecting the fairy's commands, and fearing that if he delayed she would put her threats into execution, longed to climb the beanstalk and pay the giant another visit, in order to carry away some more of his treasures; for during the time that Jack was in the giant's mansion, whilst he lay concealed in the oven, he learned from the conversation that took place between the giant and his wife that he possessed some wonderful curiosities. Jack thought of his journey again and again, but still he could not summon resolution enough to break it to his mother, being well assured that she would endeavour to prevent his going. However, one day he told her boldly that he must take a journey up the beanstalk; she begged and prayed him not to think of it, and tried all in her power to dissuade him; she told him that the giant's wife would certainly know him again, and that the giant would desire nothing better than to get him into his power, that he might put him to a cruel death in order to be revenged for the loss of his hen. Jack, finding that all his arguments were useless, pretended to give up the point, though resolved to go at all events. He had a dress prepared which would disguise him, and something to colour his skin. He thought it impossible for any one to recollect him in this dress.

A few mornings after this he arose very early, changed his complexion, and unperceived by any one, climbed the beanstalk a second time. He was greatly fatigued when he reached the top, and very hungry. Having rested some time on one of the stones, he pursued his journey to the giant's mansion. He reached it late in the evening; the woman was at the door as before. Jack addressed her, at the same time telling her a pitiful tale, and requesting that she would give him some victuals and drink and also a night's lodging.

She told him (what he knew before very well) about her husband being a powerful and cruel giant; and also that she one night admitted a poor, hungry, friendless boy, who was half dead with travelling; that the little ungrateful fellow had stolen one of the giant's treasures; and ever since that her husband had been worse than before, used her very cruelly, and continually upbraided her with being the cause of his misfortune. Jack was at no loss to discover that he was attending to the account of a story in which he was the principal actor. He did his best to persuade the good woman to admit him, but found it a very hard task. At last she consented, and as she led the way, Jack observed that everything was just as he had found it before. She took him into the kitchen, and after he had done eating and drinking, she hid him in an old lumber closet. The giant returned at the usual time, and walked in so heavily that the house was shaken to its foundation. He seated himself by the fire, and soon after exclaimed: "Wife! I smell fresh meat!" The wife replied it was the crows, who had brought a piece of raw meat and left it on the top of the house. Whilst supper was preparing the giant was very ill-tempered and impatient, frequently lifting up his hand to strike his wife for not being quick enough; she, however, was always so fortunate as to elude the blow. He was also continually upbraiding her with the loss of his wonderful hen. The giant at last having ended his voracious supper, and eaten till he was quite satisfied, said to his wife: "I must have something to amuse me; either my bags of money or my harp." After a great deal of ill-humour, and having teased his wife some time, he commanded her to bring down his bags of gold and silver. Jack, as before, peeped out of his hiding-place, and presently his wife brought two bags into the room: they were of a very large size: one was filled with new guineas, and the other with new shillings. They were both placed before the giant, who began reprimanding his poor wife most severely for staying so long; she replied, trembling with fear, that they were so heavy that she could scarcely lift them, and concluded, at last, that she would never again bring them downstairs, adding that she had nearly fainted owing to their weight. This so exasperated the giant that he raised his hand to strike her; she, however, escaped, and went to bed, leaving him to count over his treasure by way of amusement. The giant took his bags, and after turning them over and over to see that they were in the same state as he left them, began to count their contents. First, the bag which contained the silver was emptied, and the contents placed upon the table. Jack viewed the glittering heaps with delight, and most heartily wished them in his own possession. The giant (little thinking he was so narrowly watched) reckoned the silver over several times; and then, having satisfied himself that all was safe, put it into the bag again, which he made very secure. The other bag was opened next, and the guineas placed upon the table. If Jack was pleased at the sight of the silver, how much more delighted he felt when he saw such a heap of glittering gold! He even had the boldness to think of gaining both bags; but suddenly recollecting himself, he began to fear that the giant would sham sleep, the better to entrap any one who might be concealed. When the giant had counted over the gold till he was tired, he put it up, if possible more secure than he had put up the silver before; he then fell back on his chair by the fireside and fell asleep. He snored so loud that Jack compared his noise to the roaring of the sea in a high wind when the tide is coming in. At last Jack concluded him to be asleep, and therefore secure, stole out of his hiding-place, and approached the giant in order to carry off the two bags of money; but just as he laid his hand upon one of the bags, a little dog, whom he had not perceived before, started from under the giant's chair and barked at Jack most furiously, who now gave himself up for lost. Fear riveted him to the spot. Instead of endeavouring to escape, he stood still, though expecting his enemy to awake every instant. Contrary, however, to his expectation, the giant continued in a sound sleep, and the dog grew weary of barking. Jack now began to recollect himself, and on looking round saw a large piece of meat; this he threw to the dog, who instantly seized it and took it into the lumber closet which Jack had just left. Finding himself delivered from a noisy and troublesome enemy, and seeing the giant did not awake, Jack boldly seized the bags and, throwing them over his shoulders, ran out of the kitchen. He reached the street door in safety, and found it quite daylight. In his way to the top of the beanstalk, he found himself greatly incommoded with the weight of the money bags; and really they were so heavy that he could scarcely carry them. Jack was overjoyed when he found himself near the beanstalk; he soon reached the bottom, and immediately ran to seek his mother; to his great surprise the cottage was deserted; he ran from one room to another without being able to find any one; he then hastened into the village, hoping to see some of the neighbours who could inform him where he could find his mother. An old woman at last directed him to a neighbouring house, where she was ill of a fever. He was greatly shocked on finding her apparently dying, and could scarcely bear his own reflections on knowing himself to be the cause. On being informed of our hero's safe return, his mother, by degrees, revived and gradually recovered. Jack presented her with his two valuable bags. They lived happily and comfortably; the cottage was rebuilt and well furnished.

For three years Jack heard no more of the beanstalk, but he could not forget it, though he feared making his mother unhappy. She would not mention the hated beanstalk lest it should remind him of taking another journey. Notwithstanding the comforts Jack enjoyed at home, his mind dwelt continually upon the beanstalk, for the fairy's menaces, in case of his disobedience,

were ever present to his mind and prevented him from
being happy; he could think of nothing else. It was
in vain endeavouring to amuse himself; he became
thoughtful, and would arise at the first dawn of day,
and view the beanstalk for hours together. His mother
saw that something preyed heavily upon his mind,
and endeavoured to discover the cause, but Jack knew
too well what the consequence would be should she
succeed. He did his utmost, therefore, to conquer the
great desire he had for another journey up the beanstalk. Finding, however, that his inclination grew too
powerful for him, he began to make secret preparations
for his journey, and on the longest day arose as soon
as it was light, ascended the beanstalk, and reached the
top with some little trouble. He found the road, journey, etc., much as it was on the two former times; he
arrived at the giant's mansion in the evening, and
found his wife standing, as usual, at the door. Jack
had disguised himself so completely that she did not
appear to have the least recollection of him; however,
when he pleaded hunger and poverty in order to gain
admittance, he found it very difficult to persuade her.
At last he prevailed, and was concealed in the copper.
When the giant returned, he said, "I smell fresh meat!"
But Jack felt quite composed, as he had said so before
and had been soon satisfied. However, the giant
started up suddenly, and, notwithstanding all his wife

could say, he searched all round the room. Whilst this was going forward, Jack was exceedingly terrified and ready to die with fear, wishing himself at home a thousand times; but when the giant approached the copper and put his hand upon the lid, Jack thought his death was certain. The giant ended his search there without moving the lid, and seated himself quietly by the fireside. This fright nearly overcame poor Jack; he was afraid of moving or even breathing, lest he should be discovered. The giant at last ate a hearty supper. When he had finished, he commanded his wife to fetch down his harp. Jack peeped under the copper lid, and soon saw the most beautiful harp that could be imagined; it was placed by the giant on the table, who said, "Play!" and it instantly played of its own accord without being touched. The music was uncommonly fine. Jack was delighted, and felt more anxious to get the harp into his possession than either of the former treasures. The giant's soul was not attuned to harmony, and the music soon lulled him into a sound sleep. Now, therefore, was the time to carry off the harp, as the giant appeared to be in a more profound sleep than usual. Jack soon determined, got out of the copper, and seized the harp. The harp was enchanted by a fairy: it called out loudly: "Master! master!" The giant awoke, stood up, and tried to pursue Jack; but he had drunk so much that he could hardly stand. Poor Jack ran as fast as he could. In a little time the giant recovered sufficiently to walk slowly, or rather to reel after him. Had he been sober, he must have overtaken Jack instantly; but as he then was, Jack contrived to be first at the top of the beanstalk. The giant called after him in a voice like thunder, and sometimes was very near him. The moment Jack got down the beanstalk he called out for a hatchet; one was brought him directly; just at that instant the giant was beginning to descend; but Jack, with his hatchet, cut the beanstalk close off at the root, which made the giant fall headlong into the garden; the fall killed him, thereby releasing the world from a barbarous enemy. Jack's mother was delighted when she saw the beanstalk destroyed. At this instant the fairy appeared; she first addressed Jack's mother and explained every circumstance relating to the journeys up the beanstalk. The fairy charged Jack to be dutiful to his mother and to follow his father's good example, which was the only way to be happy. She then disappeared. Jack heartily begged his mother's pardon for all the sorrow and affliction he had caused her, promising most faithfully to be very dutiful and obedient to her for the future.

The Princess on the Pea

THERE was once a prince who wanted to marry a princess; but she was to be a *real* princess. So he travelled about, all through the world, to find a real one, but everywhere there was something in the way. There were princesses enough, but whether they were *real* princesses he could not quite make out; there was always something that did not seem quite right. So he came home again, and was quite sad, for he wished so much to have a real princess. One evening a terrible storm came on. It lightened and thundered, the rain streamed down; it was quite fearful! Then there was a knocking at the town gate, and the old king went out to open it.

It was a princess who stood outside the gate. But, mercy! how she looked, from the rain and the rough weather! The water ran down from her hair and her clothes; it ran in at the points of her shoes, and out at the heels; and yet she declared that she was a real princess.

"Yes, we will soon find that out," thought the old queen. But she said nothing, only went into the bed-chamber, took all the bedding off, and put a pea on the flooring of the bedstead; then she took twenty mattresses and laid them upon the pea, and then twenty eiderdown beds upon the mattresses. On this the princess had to lie all night. In the morning she was asked how she had slept.

"Oh, miserably!" said the princess. "I scarcely closed my eyes all night long. Goodness knows what was in my bed. I lay upon something hard, so that I am black and blue all over. It is quite dreadful!"

Now they saw that she was a real princess, for through the twenty mattresses and the twenty eiderdown beds she had felt the pea. No one but a real princess could be so delicate.

So the prince took her for his wife, for now he knew that he had a true princess; and the pea was put in the museum, and it is there now unless somebody has carried it off.

Look you, this is a true story.

"NOW THEY SAW THAT SHE WAS A REAL PRINCESS"

THE UGLY DUCKLING

I T WAS so glorious out in the country; it was summer; the cornfields were yellow, the oats were
green, the hay had been put up in stacks in the
green meadows, and the stork went about on his long
red legs and chattered Egyptian, for this was the
language he had learned from his good mother. All
around the fields and meadows were great forests, and
in the midst of these forests lay deep lakes. Yes, it
was right glorious out in the country. In the midst of
the sunshine there lay an old farm, with deep canals
about it, and from the wall down to the water grew
great burdocks, so high that little children could stand
upright under the loftiest of them. It was just as wild

there as in the deepest wood, and here sat a Duck upon her nest; she had to hatch her ducklings, but she was almost tired out before the little ones came and then she so seldom had visitors. The other ducks liked better to swim about in the canals than to run up to sit down under a burdock and cackle with her.

At last one egg shell after another burst open. "Piep! piep!" it cried, and in all the eggs there were little creatures that stuck out their heads.

"Quack! quack!" they said, and they all came quacking out as fast as they could, looking all round them under the green leaves, and the mother let them look as much as they chose, for green is good for the eye.

"How wide the world is!" said all the young ones, for they certainly had much more room now than when they were in the eggs.

"D'ye think this is all the world?" said the mother. "That stretches far across the other side of the garden, quite into the parson's field, but I have never been there yet. I hope you are all together," and she stood up. "No, I have not all. The largest egg still lies there. How long is that to last? I am really tired of it." And she sat down again.

"Well, how goes it?" asked an old duck who had come to pay her a visit.

"It lasts a long time with that one egg," said the Duck who sat there. "It will not burst. Now only look at the others; are they not the prettiest little ducks one could possibly see? They are all like their father. The rogue, he never comes to see me."

"Let me see the egg which will not burst," said the old visitor. "You may be sure it is a turkey's egg. I was once cheated in that way, and had much anxiety and trouble with the young ones, for they are afraid of the water. Must I say it to you, I could not get them to venture in. I quacked and I clacked, but it was no use. Let me see the egg. Yes, that's a turkey's egg. Let it lie there, and teach the other children to swim."

"I think I will sit on it a little longer," said the Duck. "I've sat so long now that I can sit a few days more."

"Just as you please," said the old duck, and she went away.

At last the great egg burst. "Piep! piep!" said the little one, and crept forth. It was very large and very ugly. The Duck looked at it.

"It's a very large duckling," said she; "none of the others look like that. Can it really be a turkey chick? Well, we shall soon find out. It must go into the water, even if I have to thrust it in myself."

The next day it was bright, beautiful weather; the sun shone on all the green trees. The Mother Duck went down to the canal with all her family. Splash! she jumped into the water. "Quack! quack!" she said, and one duckling after another plunged in. The water closed over their heads, but they came up in an instant and swam capitally; their legs went of themselves, and they were all in the water. The ugly gray Duckling swam with them.

"No, it's not a turkey," said she; "look how well it can use its legs, and how straight it holds itself. It is my own child! On the whole it's quite pretty if one looks at it rightly. Quack! quack! come with me, and I'll lead you out into the great world and present you in the duck yard; but keep close to me so that no one may tread on you, and take care of the cats!"

And so they came into the duck yard. There was a terrible riot going on in there, for two families were quarrelling about an eel's head, and the cat got it after all.

"See, that's how it goes in the world!" said the Mother Duck; and she whetted her beak, for she too wanted the eel's head. "Only use your legs," she said. "See that you can bustle about, and bow your heads before the old duck yonder. She's the grandest of all here; she's of Spanish blood—that's why she's so fat; and d'ye see? she has a red rag round her leg; that's something particularly fine, and the greatest distinction a duck can enjoy; it signifies that one does not want to lose her, and that she's to be known by the animals and by men too. Shake yourselves—don't turn in your toes; a well-brought-up duck turns its toes quite out, just like father and mother—so! Now bend your necks and say 'Quack!'"

And they did so, but the other ducks round about looked at them, and said quite boldly:

"Look there! now we're to have these hanging on, as if there were not enough of us already! And—fie!— how that duckling yonder looks; we won't stand that!" And one duck flew up at it, and bit it in the neck.

"Let it alone," said the mother; "it does no harm to any one."

"Yes, but it's too large and peculiar," said the duck who had bitten it, "and therefore it must be put down."

"Those are pretty children that the mother has there," said the old duck with the rag round her leg. "They're all pretty but that one; that was rather unlucky. I wish she could bear it over again."

"That cannot be done, my lady," replied the Mother Duck. "It is not pretty, but it has a really good disposition, and swims as well as any other; yes, I may even say it swims better. I think it will grow up pretty, and become smaller in time; it has lain too long in the egg, and therefore is not properly shaped." And then she pinched it in the neck, and smoothed its feathers. "Moreover, it is a drake," she said, "and therefore it is not of so much consequence. I think he will be very strong. He makes his way already."

"The other ducklings are graceful enough," said the old duck. "Make yourself at home; and if you find an eel's head, you may bring it me."

And now they were at home. But the poor Duckling which had crept last out of the egg and looked so ugly was bitten and pushed and jeered, as much by the ducks as by the chickens.

"It is too big!" they all said. And the turkey cock, who had been born with spurs and therefore thought himself an emperor, blew himself up like a ship in full sail, and bore straight down upon it; then he gobbled and grew quite red in the face. The poor Duckling did not know where it should stand or walk; it was quite melancholy because it looked ugly and was the butt of the whole duck yard.

So it went on the first day, and afterward it became worse and worse. The poor Duckling was hunted about by every one; even its brothers and sisters were quite angry with it, and said, "If the cat would only catch you, you ugly creature!" And the mother said, "If you were only far away!" And the ducks bit it, and the chickens beat it, and the girl who had to feed the poultry kicked at it with her foot.

Then it ran and flew over the fence, and the little birds in the bushes flew up in fear.

"That is because I am so ugly!" thought the Duckling; and it shut its eyes, but flew on farther, and so it came out into the great moor where the wild ducks lived. Here it lay the whole night long, and it was weary and downcast.

Toward morning the wild ducks flew up and looked at their new companion.

"What sort of a one are you?" they asked; and the Duckling turned in every direction and bowed as well as it could. "You are remarkably ugly!" said the wild ducks. "But that is nothing to us so long as you do not marry into our family."

Poor thing! It certainly did not think of marrying, and only hoped to obtain leave to lie among the reeds and drink some of the swamp water.

Thus it lay two whole days; then came thither two wild geese, or, properly speaking, two wild ganders. It was not long since each had crept out of an egg, and that's why they were so saucy.

"Listen, comrade," said one of them. "You're so ugly that I like you. Will you go with us and become a bird of passage? Near here, in another moor, there are a few sweet lovely wild geese, all unmarried, and all able to say 'Rap!' You've a chance of making your fortune, ugly as you are."

"Piff! paff!" resounded through the air; and the two ganders fell down dead in the swamp, and the water became blood red. "Piff! paff!" it sounded again, and the whole flock of wild geese rose up from the

57

reeds. And then there was another report. A great hunt was going on. The sportsmen were lying in wait all round the moor, and some were even sitting up in the branches of the trees, which spread far over the reeds. The blue smoke rose up like clouds among the dark trees, and was wafted far away across the water; and the hunting dogs came—splash, splash!—into the swamp, and the rushes and the reeds bent down on every side. That was a fright for the poor Duckling! It turned its head and put it under its wing; but at that moment a frightful great dog stood close by the Duckling. His tongue hung far out of his mouth, and his eyes gleamed horrible and ugly; he thrust out his nose close against the Duckling, showed his sharp teeth, and —splash, splash!—on he went without seizing it.

"Oh, Heaven be thanked!" sighed the Duckling. "I am so ugly that even the dog does not like to bite me!"

And so it lay quite quiet while the shots rattled through the reeds and gun after gun was fired. At last, late in the day, all was still; but the poor Duckling did not dare to rise up; it waited several hours before it looked round, and then hastened away out of the moor as fast as it could. It ran on over field and meadow; there was such a storm raging that it was difficult to get from one place to another.

Toward evening the Duckling came to a little miserable

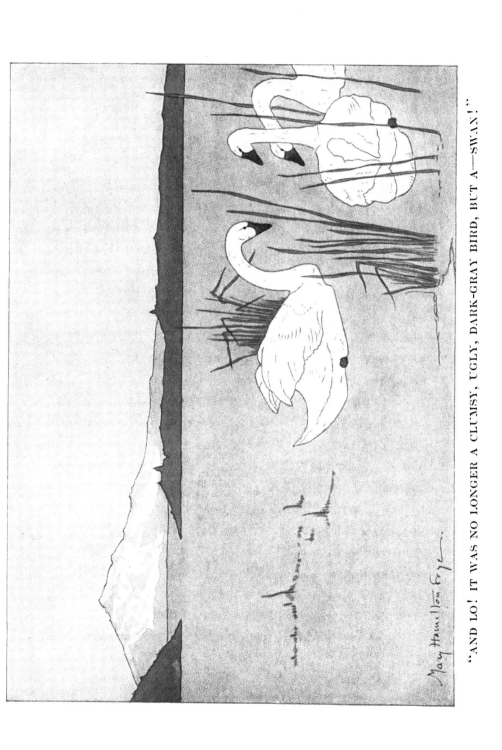

"AND LO! IT WAS NO LONGER A CLUMSY, UGLY, DARK-GRAY BIRD, BUT A—SWAN!"

peasant's hut. This hut was so dilapidated that it did not itself know on which side it should fall; and that's why it remained standing. The storm whistled round the Duckling in such a way that the poor creature was obliged to sit down, to stand against it; and the wind blew worse and worse. Then the Duckling noticed that one of the hinges of the door had given way, and the door hung so slanting that the Duckling could slip through the crack into the room; and that is what it did.

Here lived a woman, with her Cat and her Hen. And the Cat, whom she called Sonnie, could arch his back and purr, he could even give out sparks; but to make him do it one had to stroke his fur the wrong way. The Hen had quite little, short legs, and therefore she was called Chickabiddy Shortshanks. She laid good eggs, and the woman loved her like her own child.

In the morning the strange Duckling was at once noticed, and the Cat began to purr and the Hen to cluck. "What's this?" said the woman, and looked all round; but she could not see well, and therefore she thought the Duckling was a fat duck that had strayed. "This is a rare prize!" she said. "Now I shall have duck's eggs. I hope it is not a drake. We must try that."

And so the Duckling was admitted on trial for three weeks; but no eggs came. And the Cat was master of the House, and the Hen was the lady, and always said,

"We and the world!" for she thought they were half the world, and by far the better half.

The Duckling thought one might have a different opinion, but the Hen would not allow it.

"Can you lay eggs?" she asked.

"No."

"Then will you hold your tongue!"

And the Cat said, "Can you curve your back, and purr, and give out sparks?"

"No."

"Then you will please have no opinion of your own when sensible folks are speaking."

And the Duckling sat in a corner and was melancholy; then the fresh air and the sunshine streamed in, and it was seized with such a strange longing to swim on the water, that it could not help telling the Hen of it.

"What are you thinking of?" cried the Hen. "You have nothing to do, that's why you have these fancies. Lay eggs, or purr, and they will pass over."

"But it is so charming to swim on the water!" said the Duckling, "so refreshing to let it close above one's head, and to dive down to the bottom."

"Yes, that must be a mighty pleasure, truly," quoth the Hen, "I fancy you must have gone crazy. Ask the Cat about it—he's the cleverest animal I know—ask him if he likes to swim on the water, or to dive down— I won't speak about myself. Ask our mistress, the old woman; no one in the world is cleverer than she. Do you think she has any desire to swim, and to let the water close above her head?"

"You don't understand me," said the Duckling.

"We don't understand you? Then pray who is to understand you? You surely don't pretend to be cleverer than the Cat and the woman—I won't say anything of myself. Don't be conceited, child, and thank your Maker for all the kindness you have received. Did you not get into a warm room, and have you not fallen into company from which you may learn something? But you are a chatterer, and it is not pleasant to associate with you. You may believe me, I speak for your good. I tell you disagreeable things, and by that one may always know one's true friends! Only take care that you learn to lay eggs, or to purr and give out sparks!"

"I think I will go out into the wide world," said the Duckling.

"Yes, do go," replied the Hen.

And so the Duckling went away. It swam on the water and dived, but it was slighted by every creature because of its ugliness.

Now came the autumn. The leaves in the forest turned yellow and brown; the wind caught them so that they danced about, and up in the air it was very cold. The clouds hung low, heavy with hail and snowflakes, and on the fence stood the raven, crying, "Croak! croak!" for mere cold; yes, it was enough to make one feel cold to think of this. The poor little Duckling certainly had not a good time. One evening—the sun was just setting in his beauty—there came a whole flock of great, handsome birds out of the bushes. They were dazzlingly white, with long, flexible necks—they were swans. They uttered a very peculiar cry, spread forth their glorious great wings, and flew away from that cold region to warmer lands, to fair open lakes. They mounted so high, so high! and the ugly Duckling felt quite strangely as it watched them. It turned round and round in the water like a wheel, stretched out its neck toward them, and uttered such a strange loud cry as frightened itself. Oh! it could not forget those beautiful, happy birds; and as soon as it could see them no longer it dived down to the very bottom, and when it came up again it was quite beside itself. It knew not the name of those birds, and knew not whither they were flying, but it loved them more than it had ever loved any one. It was not at all envious of them. How could it think of wishing to possess such loveliness as they had? It would have been glad if only the ducks would have endured its company—the poor, ugly creature!

And the winter grew cold, very cold! The Duckling was forced to swim about in the water to prevent the surface from freezing entirely; but every night the hole in which it swam about became smaller and smaller. It froze so hard that the icy covering crackled again; and the Duckling was obliged to use its legs continually to prevent the hole from freezing up. At last it became exhausted, and lay quite still, and thus froze fast into the ice.

Early in the morning a peasant came by, and when he saw what had happened, he took his wooden shoe, broke the ice crust to pieces, and carried the Duckling home to his wife. Then it came to itself again. The children wanted to play with it, but the Duckling thought they wanted to hurt it, and in its terror fluttered up into the milkpan, so that the milk spurted down into the room. The woman clasped her hands, at which the Duckling flew down into the butter-tub, and then into the meal-barrel and out again. How it looked then! The woman screamed, and struck at it with the firetongs; the children tumbled over one another in their efforts to catch the Duckling; and they laughed and they screamed!—well it was that the door stood open, and the poor creature was able to slip out between the shrubs into the newly fallen snow—there it lay quite exhausted.

But it would be too melancholy if I were to tell all the misery and care which the Duckling had to endure in the hard winter. It lay out on the moor among the reeds when the sun began to shine again and the larks to sing. It was a beautiful spring.

Then all at once the Duckling could flap its wings. They beat the air more strongly than before, and bore it rapidly away; and before it well knew how all this happened, it found itself in a great garden, where the elder trees smelt sweet, and bent their long green branches down to the canal that wound through the region. Oh, here it was so beautiful, such a gladness of spring; and from the thicket came three glorious white swans; they rustled their wings and swam lightly on the water. The Duckling knew the splendid creatures, and felt oppressed by a peculiar sadness.

"I will fly away to them, to the royal birds, and they will beat me because I, that am so ugly, dare to come near them. But it is all the same. Better to be killed by *them* than to be pursued by ducks, and beaten by fowls, and pushed about by the girl who takes care of the poultry yard, and to suffer hunger in winter!" And it flew out into the water, and swam toward the beautiful swans; these looked at it, and came sailing down upon it with outspread wings. "Kill me!" said the poor creature, and bent its head down upon the water, expecting nothing but death. But what was this that it saw in the clear water? It beheld its own image; and lo! it was no longer a clumsy dark-gray bird, ugly and hateful to look at, but a—swan!

THE UGLY DUCKLING

It matters nothing if one is born in a duck yard if one has only lain in a swan's egg.

It felt quite glad at all the need and misfortune it had suffered; now it realized its happiness in all the splendour that surrounded it. And the great swans swam round it, and stroked it with their beaks.

Into the garden came little children, who threw bread and corn into the water; and the youngest cried, "There is a new one!" and the other children shouted joyously, "Yes, a new one has arrived!" And they clapped their hands and danced about, and ran to their father and mother; and bread and cake were thrown into the water; and they all said, "The new one is the most beautiful of all! so young and handsome!" and the old swans bowed their heads before him. Then he felt quite ashamed, and hid his head under his wings, for he did not know what to do he was so happy, and yet not at all proud. He thought how he had been persecuted and despised, and now he heard them saying that he was the most beautiful of all birds. Even the elder tree bent its branches straight down into the water before him, and the sun shone warm and mild. Then his wings rustled, he lifted his slender neck, and cried rejoicingly from the depths of his heart:

"I never dreamed of so much happiness when I was the ugly Duckling!"

THE LIGHT PRINCESS

I

What! No Children?

ONCE upon a time, so long ago that I have quite forgotten the date, there lived a king and queen who had no children.

And the king said to himself, "All the queens of my acquaintance have children, some three, some seven, and some as many as twelve; and my queen has not one. I feel ill-used." So he made up his mind to be cross with his wife about it. But she bore it all like a good patient queen as she was. Then the king grew very cross indeed, but the queen pretended to take it all as a joke, and a very good one, too.

"Why don't you have any daughters, at least?" said he. "I don't say *sons;* that might be too much to expect."

"I am sure, dear king, I am very sorry," said the queen.

"So you ought to be," retorted the king; "you are not going to make a virtue of *that,* surely."

But he was not an ill-tempered king, and in any matter of less moment would have let the queen have her own way with all his heart. This, however, was an affair of State.

The queen smiled.

"You must have patience with a lady, you know, dear king," said she.

She was, indeed, a very nice queen, and heartily sorry that she could not oblige the king immediately.

The king tried to have patience, but he succeeded very badly. It was more than he deserved, therefore, when, at last, the queen gave him a daughter—as lovely a little princess as ever cried.

II

Won't I, Just?

The day drew near when the infant must be christened. The king wrote all the invitations with his own hand. Of course somebody was forgotten.

Now it does not generally matter if somebody *is* forgotten, only you must mind who. Unfortunately, the king forgot without intending to forget; and so the chance fell upon the Princess Makemnoit, which was awkward, for the princess was the king's own sister, and he ought not to have forgotten her. But she had made herself so disagreeable to the old king, their father, that he had forgotten her in making his will; and so it was no wonder that her brother forgot her in writing his invitations. But poor relations don't do anything to keep you in mind of them. Why don't they? The king could not see into the garret she lived in, could he?

She was a sour, spiteful creature. The wrinkles of contempt crossed the wrinkles of peevishness, and made her face as full of wrinkles as a pat of butter. If ever a king could be justified in forgetting anybody, this king was justified in forgetting his sister, even at a christening. She looked very odd, too. Her forehead was as large as all the rest of her face, and projected over it like a precipice. When she was angry her little eyes flashed blue. When she hated anybody they shone yellow and green. What they looked like when she loved anybody I do not know, for I never heard of her loving anybody but herself, and I do not think she could have managed that if she had not somehow got used to herself. But what made it highly imprudent in the king to forget her was—that she was awfully clever. In fact, she was a witch; and when she bewitched anybody, he very soon had enough of it, for she beat all the wicked fairies in wickedness, and all the clever ones in cleverness. She despised all the modes we read of in history, in which offended fairies and witches have taken their revenges; and therefore, after waiting and waiting in vain for an invitation, she made up her mind at last to go without one and make the whole family miserable, like a princess as she was.

So she put on her best gown, went to the palace, was kindly received by the happy monarch, who forgot that he had forgotten her, and took her place in the procession to the royal chapel. When they were all gathered about the font, she contrived to get next to it and throw something into the water, after which she maintained a very respectful demeanour till the water was applied to the child's face. But at that moment she turned round in her place three times, and muttered the following words, loud enough for those beside her to hear:

> "Light of spirit, by my charms,
> Light of body, every part,
> Never weary human arms—
> Only crush thy parents' heart!"

They all thought she had lost her wits and was repeating some foolish nursery rhyme; but a shudder went through the whole of them notwithstanding. The baby, on the contrary, began to laugh and crow, while the nurse gave a start and a smothered cry, for she thought she was struck with paralysis: she could not feel the baby in her arms. But she clasped it tight and said nothing.

The mischief was done.

III

She Can't Be Ours!

Her atrocious aunt had deprived the child of all her gravity. If you ask me how this was effected, I answer, "In the easiest way in the world. She had only to destroy gravitation." For the princess was a philosopher, and knew all the ins and outs of the laws of gravitation as well as the ins and outs of her boot-lace. And being a witch as well, she could abrogate those laws in a moment, or at least so clog their wheels and rust their bearings that they would not work at all. But we have more to do with what followed than with how it was done.

The first awkwardness that resulted from this unhappy privation was that the moment the nurse began to float the baby up and down, she flew from her arms toward the ceiling. Happily, the resistance of the air brought her ascending career to a close within a foot of it. There she remained, horizontal as when she left the nurse's arms, kicking and laughing amazingly. The nurse in terror flew to the bell, and begged the footman, who answered it, to bring up the house-steps directly. Trembling in every limb, she climbed upon the steps, and had to stand upon the very top and reach up before she could catch the floating tail of the baby's long clothes.

When the strange fact came to be known, there was a terrible commotion in the palace. The occasion of its discovery by the king was naturally a repetition of the nurse's experience. Astonished that he felt no weight when the child was laid in his arms, he began to wave her up and—not down; for she slowly ascended to the ceiling as before, and there remained floating in perfect comfort and satisfaction, as was testified by her peals of tiny laughter. The king stood staring up in speechless amazement, and trembled so that his beard shook like grass in the wind. At last, turning to the queen, who was just as horror-struck as himself, he said, gasping, staring, and stammering:

"She *can't* be ours, queen!"

Now the queen was much cleverer than the king, and had begun already to suspect that "this effect defective came by cause."

"I am sure she is ours," answered she. "But we ought to have taken better care of her at the christening. People who were never invited ought not to have been present."

"Oh, ho!" said the king, tapping his forehead with his forefinger, "I have it all. I've found her out. Don't you see it, queen? Princess Makemnoit has bewitched her."

"That's just what I say," answered the queen.

"I beg your pardon, my love; I did not hear you. John! bring the steps I get on my throne with."

For he was a little king with a great throne, like many other kings.

The throne steps were brought and set upon the dining-table, and John got upon the top of them. But he could not reach the little princess, who lay like a baby-laughter cloud in the air, exploding continuously.

"Take the tongs, John," said his Majesty; and getting up on the table, he handed them to him.

John could reach the baby now, and the little princess was handed down by the tongs.

IV

Where Is She?

One fine summer day, a month after these her first adventures, during which time she had been very carefully watched, the princess was lying on the bed in the queen's own chamber, fast asleep. One of the windows was open, for it was noon, and the day was so sultry that the little girl was wrapped in nothing less ethereal than slumber itself. The queen came into the room, and not observing that the baby was on the bed, opened another window. A frolicsome fairy wind, which had been watching for a chance of mischief, rushed in at the one window, and taking its way over the bed where the child was lying, caught her up, and rolling and floating her along like a piece of flue or a dandelion seed, carried her with it through the opposite window and away. The queen went downstairs, quite ignorant of the loss she had herself occasioned.

When the nurse returned, she supposed that her Majesty had carried her off and, dreading a scolding, delayed making inquiry about her. But hearing nothing she grew uneasy and went at length to the queen's boudoir, where she found her Majesty.

"Please, your Majesty, shall I take the baby?" said she.

"Where is she?" asked the queen.

"Please forgive me. I know it was wrong."

"What do you mean?" said the queen, looking grave.

"Oh! don't frighten me, your Majesty!" exclaimed the nurse, clasping her hands.

The queen saw that something was amiss, and fell down in a faint. The nurse rushed about the palace, screaming, "My baby! my baby!"

Every one ran to the queen's room. But the queen could give no orders. They soon found out, however, that the princess was missing, and in a moment the palace was like a beehive in a garden; and in one minute more the queen was brought to herself by a great shout and a clapping of hands. They had found the princess fast asleep under a rosebush, to which the elfish little wind-puff had carried her, finishing its mischief by shaking a shower of red rose leaves all over the little white sleeper. Startled by the noise the servants made, she woke and, filled with glee, scattered the rose leaves in all directions like a shower of spray in the sunset.

She was watched more carefully after this, no doubt; yet it would be endless to relate all the odd incidents resulting from this peculiarity of the young princess. But there never was a baby in a house, not to say a palace, that kept the household in such constant good humour, at least below-stairs. If it was not easy for her nurses to hold her, at least she made neither their arms nor their hearts ache. And she was so nice to play ball with! There was positively no danger of letting her fall. They might throw her down, or knock her down, or push her down, but they couldn't *let* her down. It is true, they might let her fly into the fire or the coal hole or through the window, but none of these accidents had happened as yet. If you heard peals of laughter resounding from some unknown region, you might be sure enough of the cause. Going down into the kitchen, or *the room*, you would find Jane and Thomas and Robert and Susan, all and sum, playing at ball with the little princess. She was the ball herself, and did not enjoy it the less for that. Away she went, flying from one to another, screeching with laughter. And the servants loved the ball itself better even than the game. But they had to take some care how they threw her, for if she received an upward direction, she would never come down again without being fetched.

V

What Is To Be Done?

But above-stairs it was different. One day, for instance, after breakfast the king went into his counting-house, and counted out his money.

The operation gave him no pleasure.

"To think," said he to himself, "that every one of these gold sovereigns weighs a quarter of an ounce, and my real, live, flesh-and-blood princess weighs nothing at all!"

And he hated his gold sovereigns, as they lay with a broad smile of self-satisfaction all over their yellow faces.

The queen was in the parlour, eating bread and

honey. But at the second mouthful she burst out crying, and could not swallow it. The king heard her sobbing. Glad of anybody, but especially of his queen, to quarrel with, he clashed his gold sovereigns into his money box, clapped his crown on his head, and rushed into the parlour.

"What is all this about?" exclaimed he. "What are you crying for, queen?"

"I can't eat it," said the queen, looking ruefully at the honey pot.

"No wonder!" retorted the king. "You've just eaten your breakfast—two turkey eggs and three anchovies."

"Oh, that's not it!" sobbed her Majesty. "It's my child, my child!"

"Well, what's the matter with your child? She's neither up the chimney nor down the draw-well. Just hear her laughing."

Yet the king could not help a sigh, which he tried to turn into a cough, saying:

"It is a good thing to be light-hearted, I am sure, whether she be ours or not."

"It is a bad thing to be light-headed," answered the queen looking with prophetic soul far into the future.

"'Tis a good thing to be light-handed," said the king.

"'Tis a bad thing to be light-fingered," answered the queen.

"'Tis a good thing to be light-footed," said the king.

"'Tis a bad thing——" began the queen; but the king interrupted her.

"In fact," said he, with the tone of one who concludes an argument in which he has had only imaginary opponents, and in which, therefore, he has come off triumphant—"in fact, it is a good thing altogether to be light-bodied."

"But it is a bad thing altogether to be light-minded," retorted the queen, who was beginning to lose her temper.

This last answer quite discomfited his Majesty, who turned on his heel and betook himself to his countinghouse again. But he was not halfway toward it when the voice of his queen overtook him.

"And it's a bad thing to be light-haired," screamed she, determined to have more last words now that her spirit was roused.

The queen's hair was black as night; and the king's had been, and his daughter's was, golden as morning. But it was not this reflection on his hair that arrested him; it was the double use of the word *light*, for the king hated all witticisms, and punning especially. And besides, he could not tell whether the queen meant light-*haired* or light-*heired*, for why might she not aspirate her vowels when she was exasperated herself?

He turned upon his other heel, and rejoined her. She looked angry still, because she knew that she was guilty, or, what was much the same, knew that he thought so.

"My dear queen," said he, "duplicity of any sort is exceedingly objectionable between married people of any rank, not to say kings and queens; and the most objectionable **form** duplicity can assume is that of punning."

"There!" said the queen, "I never made a jest but I broke it in the making. I am the most unfortunate woman in the world!"

She looked so rueful that the king took her in his arms, and they sat down to consult.

"Can you bear this?" said the king.

"No, I can't," said the queen.

"Well, what's to be done?" said the king.

"I'm sure I don't know," said the queen. "But might you not try an apology?"

"To my old sister, I suppose you mean?" said the king.

"Yes," said the queen.

"Well, I don't mind," said the king.

So he went the next morning to the house of the princess, and making a very humble apology, begged her to undo the spell. But the princess declared, with a grave face, that she knew nothing at all about it. Her eyes, however, shone pink, which was a sign that she was happy. She advised the king and queen to have patience and to mend their ways. The king returned disconsolate. The queen tried to comfort him.

"We will wait till she is older. She may then be able to suggest something herself. She will know at least how she feels, and explain things to us."

"But what if she should marry?" exclaimed the king, in sudden consternation at the idea.

"Well, what of that?" rejoined the queen.

"Just think! If she were to have children! In the course of a hundred years the air might be as full of floating children as of gossamers in autumn."

"That is no business of ours," replied the queen. "Besides, by that time they will have learned to take care of themselves."

A sigh was the king's only answer.

He would have consulted the court physicians, but he was afraid they would try experiments upon her.

VI

She Laughs Too Much

Meantime, notwithstanding awkward occurrences, and griefs that she brought upon her parents, the little princess laughed and grew—not fat, but plump and tall. She reached the age of seventeen without having fallen into any worse scrape than a chimney, by rescuing her from which a little bird-nesting urchin got fame and a black face. Nor, thoughtless as she was, had she committed anything worse than laughter at everybody and everything that came in her way. When she was told, for the sake of experiment, that General Clanrunfort was cut to pieces with all his troops, she laughed; when she heard that the enemy was on his way to besiege her father's capital, she laughed hugely; but when she was told that the city would certainly be abandoned to the mercy of the enemy's soldiery—why, then she laughed immoderately. She never could be brought to see the serious side of anything. When her mother cried, she said:

"What queer faces mamma makes! And she squeezes water out of her cheeks! Funny mamma!"

And when her papa stormed at her, she laughed and danced round and round him, clapping her hands and crying:

"Do it again, papa. Do it again! It's such fun! Dear, funny papa!"

And if he tried to catch her, she glided from him in an instant, not in the least afraid of him, but thinking it part of the game not to be caught. With one push of her foot she would be floating in the air above his head; or she would go dancing backward and forward and sideways, like a great butterfly. It happened several times, when her father and mother were holding a consultation about her in private, that they were interrupted by vainly repressed outbursts of laughter over their heads; and looking up with indignation, saw her floating at full length in the air above them, whence she regarded them with the most comical appreciation of the position.

One day an awkward accident happened. The princess had come out upon the lawn with one of her attendants, who held her by the hand. Spying her father at the other side of the lawn, she snatched her hand from the maid's and sped across to him. Now when she wanted to run alone, her custom was to catch up a stone in each hand, so that she might come down again after a bound. Whatever she wore as part of her attire had no effect in this way. Even gold, when it thus became as it were a part of herself, lost all its weight for the time. But whatever she only held in her hands retained its downward tendency. On this occasion she could see nothing to catch up but a huge toad that was walking across the lawn as if he had a hundred years to do it in. Not knowing what disgust meant, for this was one of her peculiarities, she snatched up the toad and bounded away. She had almost reached her father, and he was holding out his arms to receive her and take from her lips the kiss which hovered on them like a butterfly on a rosebud, when a puff of wind blew her aside into the arms of a young page, who had just been receiving a message from his Majesty. Now it was no great peculiarity in the princess that, once she was set agoing, it always cost her time and trouble to check herself.   On this occasion there was no time. She *must* kiss—and she kissed the page.   She did not mind it much, for she had no shyness in her composition; and she knew, besides, that she could not help it.   So she only laughed like a musical box.   The poor page fared the worst, for the princess, trying to correct the unfortunate tendency of the kiss, put out her hands to keep off the page; so that, along with the kiss, he received, on the other cheek, a slap with the huge black toad, which she poked right into his eye.   He tried to laugh, too, but the attempt resulted in such an odd contortion of countenance as showed that there was no danger of his pluming himself on the kiss.   As for the king, his dignity was greatly hurt and he did not speak to the page for a whole month.

I may here remark that it was very amusing to see her run, if her mode of progression could properly be called running, for first she would make a bound, then, having alighted, she would run a few steps and make another bound.   Sometimes she would fancy she had reached the ground before she actually had, and her feet would go backward and forward, running upon nothing at all, like those of a chicken on its back.   Then she would laugh like the very spirit of fun, only in her laugh there was something missing.   What it was, I find myself unable to describe. I think it was a certain tone, depending upon the possibility of sorrow—*morbidezza*, perhaps. She never smiled.

VII

Try Metaphysics

After a long avoidance of the painful subject, the king and queen resolved to hold a council of three upon it, and so they sent for the princess. In she came, sliding and flitting and gliding from one piece of furniture to another, and put herself at last in an armchair, in a sitting posture. Whether she could be said *to sit*, seeing she received no support from the seat of the chair, I do not pretend to determine.

"My dear child," said the king, "you must be aware by this time that you are not exactly like other people."

"Oh, you dear funny papa! I have got a nose, and two eyes, and all the rest. So have you. So has mamma."

"Now be serious, my dear, for once," said the queen.

"No, thank you, mamma; I had rather not."

"Would you not like to be able to walk like other people?" said the king.

"No indeed, I should think not. You only crawl. You are such slow coaches!"

"How do you feel, my child?" he resumed, after a pause of discomfiture.

"Quite well, thank you."

"I mean, what do you feel like?"

"Like nothing at all that I know of."

"You must feel like something."

"I feel like a princess with such a funny papa and such a dear pet of a queen-mamma!"

"Now really!" began the queen, but the princess interrupted her.

"Oh, yes," she added, "I remember. I have a curious feeling sometimes, as if I were the only person that had any sense in the whole world."

She had been trying to behave herself with dignity, but now she burst into a violent fit of laughter, threw herself backward over the chair, and went rolling about the floor in an ecstasy of enjoyment. The king picked her up easier than one does a down quilt, and replaced her in her former relation to the chair. The exact preposition expressing this relation I do not happen to know.

"Is there nothing you wish for?" resumed the king, who had learned by this time that it was useless to be angry with her.

"Oh, you dear papa!—yes," answered she.

"What is it, my darling?"

"I have been longing for it—oh, such a time!—ever since last night."

"Tell me what it is."

"Will you promise to let me have it?"

The king was on the point of saying yes, but the wiser queen checked him with a single motion of her head.

"Tell me what it is first," said he.

"No, no. Promise first."

"I dare not. What is it?"

"Mind, I hold you to your promise. It is—to be tied to the end of a string—a very long string indeed, and be flown like a kite. Oh, such fun! I would rain rose water, and hail sugar plums, and snow whipped cream, and—and—and——"

A fit of laughing checked her, and she would have been off again over the floor, had not the king started up and caught her just in time. Seeing that nothing but talk could be got out of her, he rang the bell, and sent her away with two of her ladies-in-waiting.

"Now, queen," he said, turning to her Majesty, "what *is* to be done?"

"There is but one thing left," answered she. "Let us consult the College of Metaphysicians."

"Bravo!" cried the king, "we will."

Now at the head of this college were two very wise Chinese philosophers—by name Hum-Drum and Kopy-Keck. For them the king sent, and straightway they came. In a long speech he communicated to them what they knew very well already—as who did not?—

namely, the peculiar condition of his daughter in relation to the globe on which she dwelt; and requested them to consult together as to what might be the cause and probable cure of her *infirmity*. The king laid stress upon the word, but failed to discover his own pun. The queen laughed, but Hum-Drum and Kopy-Keck heard with humility and retired in silence.

Their consultation consisted chiefly in propounding and supporting, for the thousandth time, each his favourite theories. For the condition of the princess afforded delightful scope for the discussion of every question arising from the division of thought—in fact, of all the metaphysics of the Chinese Empire. But it is only justice to say that they did not altogether neglect the discussion of the practical question, *what was to be done.*

Hum-Drum was a Materialist, and Kopy-Keck was a Spiritualist. The former was slow and sententious; the latter was quick and flighty; the latter had generally the first word; the former the last.

"I reassert my former assertion," began Kopy-Keck, with a plunge. "There is not a fault in the princess, body or soul, only they are wrong put together. Listen to me now, Hum-Drum, and I will tell you in brief what I think. Don't speak. Don't answer me. I *won't* hear you till I have done. At that decisive moment when souls seek their appointed habitations, two eager souls met, struck, rebounded, lost their way, and arrived each at the wrong place. The soul of the princess was one of those, and she went far astray. She does not belong by rights to this world at all, but to some other planet, probably Mercury. Her proclivity to her true sphere destroys all the natural influence which this orb would otherwise possess over her corporeal frame. She cares for nothing here. There is no relation between her and this world.

"She must therefore be taught, by the sternest compulsion, to take an interest in the earth as the earth. She must study every department of its history—its animal history, its vegetable history, its mineral history, its social history, its moral history, its political history, its scientific history, its literary history, its musical history, its artistical history, above all, its metaphysical history. She must begin with the Chinese dynasty and end with Japan. But first of all she must study geology and especially the history of the extinct races of animals —their natures, their habits, their loves, their hates, their revenges. She must——"

"Hold, h-o-o-old!" roared Hum-Drum. "It is certainly my turn now. My rooted and insubvertible conviction is that the causes of the anomalies evident in the princess's condition are strictly and solely physical. But that is only tantamount to acknowledging that they exist. Hear my opinion. From some cause or other, of no importance to our inquiry, the motion of her heart has been reversed. That remarkable combination of the suction and the force pump works the wrong way—I mean in the case of the unfortunate princess it draws in where it should force out, and forces out where it should draw in. The offices of the auricles and the ventricles are subverted. The blood is sent forth by the veins and returns by the arteries. Consequently it is running the wrong way through all her corporeal organism—lungs and all. Is it then at all mysterious, seeing that such is the case, that on the other particular of gravitation as well she should differ from normal humanity? My proposal for the cure is this:

"Phlebotomize until she is reduced to the last point of safety. Let it be effected, if necessary, in a warm bath. When she is reduced to a state of perfect asphyxy, apply a ligature to the left ankle, drawing it as tight as the bone will bear. Apply, at the same moment, another of equal tension around the right wrist. By means of plates constructed for the purpose, place the other foot and hand under the receivers of two air-pumps. Exhaust the receivers. Exhibit a pint of French brandy, and await the result."

"Which would presently arrive in the form of grim Death," said Kopy-Keck.

"If it should, she would yet die in doing our duty," retorted Hum-Drum.

But their Majesties had too much tenderness for their volatile offspring to subject her to either of the schemes of the equally unscrupulous philosophers. Indeed, the most complete knowledge of the laws of nature would have been unserviceable in her case, for it was impossible to classify her. She was a fifth imponderable body sharing all the other properties of the ponderable.

VIII

Try a Drop of Water

Perhaps the best thing for the princess would have been to fall in love. But how a princess who had no gravity could fall into anything is a difficulty—perhaps *the* difficulty. As for her own feeling on the subject, she did not even know that there was such a beehive of honey and stings to be fallen into. But now I come to mention another curious fact about her.

The palace was built on the shores of the loveliest lake in the world, and the princess loved this lake more than father or mother. The root of this preference no doubt, although the princess did not recognize it as such, was that the moment she got into it she recovered the natural right of which she had been so wickedly deprived—namely, gravity. Whether this was owing to the fact that water had been employed as the means of conveying the injury, I do not know, but it is certain that she could swim and dive like the duck that her old nurse said she was. The manner in which this alleviation of her misfortune was discovered was as follows:

One summer evening, during the carnival of the country, she had been taken upon the lake by the king and queen, in the royal barge. They were accompanied by many of the courtiers in a fleet of little boats. In the middle of the lake she wanted to get into the lord chancellor's barge, for his daughter, who was a great favourite with her, was in it with her father. Now though the old king rarely condescended to make light of his misfortune, yet, happening on this occasion to be in a particularly good humour, as the barges approached each other he caught up the princess to throw her into the chancellor's barge. He lost his balance, however, and dropping into the bottom of the barge, lost his hold of his daughter; not, however, before imparting to her the downward tendency of his own person, though in a somewhat different direction, for as the king fell into the boat, she fell into the water. With a burst of delighted laughter she disappeared into the lake. A cry of horror ascended from the boats. They had never seen the princess go down before. Half the men were under water in a moment; but they had all, one after another, come up to the surface again for breath, when —tinkle, tinkle, babble, and gush! came the princess's laugh over the water from far away. There she was, swimming like a swan. Nor would she come out for king or queen, chancellor or daughter. She was perfectly obstinate.

But at the same time she seemed more sedate than usual. Perhaps that was because a great pleasure spoils laughing. At all events, after this the passion of her life was to get into the water, and she was always the better behaved and the more beautiful the more she had of it. Summer and winter it was quite the same, only she could not stay so long in the water when they had to break the ice to let her in. Any day, from morning to evening in summer, she might be descried—a streak of white in the blue water—lying as still as the shadow of a cloud or shooting along like a dolphin, disappearing and coming up again far off, just where one did not expect her. She would have been in the lake of a night, too, if she could have had her way, for the balcony of her window overhung a deep pool in it, and through a shallow reedy passage she could have swam out into the wide wet water, and no one would have been any the wiser. Indeed, when she happened to wake in the moonlight she could hardly resist the temptation. But there was the sad difficulty of getting into it. She had as great a dread of the air as some children have of the water. For the slightest gust of wind would blow her away, and a gust might arise in the stillest moment. And if she gave herself a push toward the water and just failed of reaching it, her situation would be dreadfully awkward, irrespective of the wind; for at best there she would have to remain, suspended in her nightgown, till she was seen and angled for by somebody from the window.

"Oh! if I had my gravity," thought she, contemplating the water. "I would flash off this balcony like a long white seabird, headlong into the darling wetness. Heigh-ho!"

This was the only consideration that made her wish to be like other people.

Another reason for her being fond of the water was that in it alone she enjoyed any freedom, for she could not walk without a *cortège*, consisting in part of a troop of light horse, for fear of the liberties which the wind might take with her. And the king grew more apprehensive with increasing years, till at last he would not allow her to walk abroad at all without some twenty silken cords fastened to as many parts of her dress and held by twenty noblemen. Of course horseback was out of the question. But she bade good-bye to all this ceremony when she got into the water.

And so remarkable were its effects upon her, especially in restoring her for the time to the ordinary human gravity, that Hum-Drum and Kopy-Keck agreed in recommending the king to bury her alive for three years; in the hope that as the water did her so much good, the earth would do her yet more. But the king had some vulgar prejudices against the experiment, and would not give his consent. Foiled in this, they yet agreed in another recommendation, which, seeing that one imported his opinions from China and the other from Thibet, was very remarkable indeed. They argued that if water of external origin and application could be so efficacious, water from a deeper source might work a perfect cure; in short, that if the poor afflicted princess could by any means be made to cry, she might recover her lost gravity.

But how was this to be brought about? Therein lay all the difficulty—to meet which the philosophers were not wise enough. To make the princess cry was as impossible as to make her weigh. They sent for a professional beggar, commanded him to prepare his most touching oracle of woe, helped him out of the court charade box to whatever he wanted for dressing up, and promised great rewards in the event of his success. But it was all in vain. She listened to the mendicant artist's story, and gazed at his marvellous make-up, till she could contain herself no longer and went into the most undignified contortions for relief, shrieking, positively screeching, with laughter.

When she had a little recovered herself, she ordered her attendants to drive him away and not give him a

single copper; whereupon his look of mortified discomfiture wrought her punishment and his revenge,
for it sent her into violent hysterics, from which she was
with difficulty recovered.

But so anxious was the king that the suggestion
should have a fair trial, that he put himself in a rage one
day, and rushing up to her room, gave her an awful
whipping. Yet not a tear would flow. She looked
grave, and her laughing sounded uncommonly like
screaming—that was all. The good old tyrant, though
he put on his best gold spectacles to look, could not
discover the smallest cloud in the serene blue of her
eyes.

IX

Put Me in Again!

It must have been about this time that the son of
a king, who lived a thousand miles from Lagobel, set
out to look for the daughter of a queen. He travelled
far and wide, but as sure as he found a princess, he
found some fault with her. Of course he could not
marry a mere woman, however beautiful, and there was
no princess to be found worthy of him. Whether the
prince was so near perfection that he had a right to demand perfection itself, I cannot pretend to say. All I
know is, that he was a fine, handsome, brave, generous,
well-bred, and well-behaved youth, as all princes are.

THE LIGHT PRINCESS

In his wanderings he had come across some reports about our princess; but as everybody said she was bewitched, he never dreamed that she could bewitch him. For what indeed could a prince do with a princess that had lost her gravity? Who could tell what she might not lose next? She might lose her visibility, or her tangibility, or, in short, the power of making impressions upon the radical sensorium, so that he should never be able to tell whether she was dead or alive. Of course he made no further inquiries about her.

One day he lost sight of his retinue in a great forest. These forests are very useful in delivering princes from their courtiers, like a sieve that keeps back the bran. Then the princes get away to follow their fortunes. In this way they have the advantage of the princesses, who are forced to marry before they have had a bit of fun. I wish our princesses got lost in a forest sometimes.

One lovely evening, after wandering about for many days, he found that he was approaching the outskirts of this forest; for the trees had got so thin that he could see the sunset through them, and he soon came upon a kind of heath. Next he came upon signs of human neighbourhood; but by this time it was getting late, and there was nobody in the fields to direct him.

After travelling for another hour, his horse, quite worn out with long labour and lack of food, fell and was

unable to rise again. So he continued his journey on
foot. At length he entered another wood—not a wild
forest, but a civilized wood, through which a footpath
led him to the side of a lake. Along this path the prince
pursued his way through the gathering darkness. Suddenly he paused and listened. Strange sounds came
across the water. It was, in fact, the princess laughing.
Now there was something odd in her laugh, as I have
already hinted, for the hatching of a real hearty laugh
requires the incubation of gravity; and perhaps this
was how the prince mistook the laughter for screaming.
Looking over the lake, he saw something white in the
water, and in an instant he had torn off his tunic,
kicked off his sandals, and plunged in. He soon
reached the white object and found that it was a
woman. There was not light enough to show that she
was a princess, but quite enough to show that she was
a lady, for it does not want much light to see that.

Now I cannot tell how it came about—whether she
pretended to be drowning, or whether he frightened
her, or caught her so as to embarrass her—but certainly he brought her to shore in a fashion ignominious
to a swimmer, and more nearly drowned than she had
ever expected to be, for the water had got into her
throat as often as she had tried to speak.

At the place to which he bore her, the bank was only
a foot or two above the water; so he gave her a strong

lift out of the water to lay her on the bank. But her gravitation ceasing the moment she left the water, away she went up into the air, scolding and screaming.

"You naughty, *naughty*, NAUGHTY, NAUGHTY man!" she cried.

No one had ever succeeded in putting her into a passion before. When the prince saw her ascend, he thought he must have been bewitched, and have mistaken a great swan for a lady. But the princess caught hold of the topmost cone upon a lofty fir. This came off, but she caught at another, and in fact stopped herself by gathering cones, dropping them as the stalks gave way. The prince, meantime, stood in the water staring and forgetting to get out. But the princess disappearing, he scrambled on shore and went in the direction of the tree. There he found her climbing down one of the branches toward the stem. But in the darkness of the wood, the prince continued in some bewilderment as to what the phenomenon could be; until, reaching the ground, and seeing him standing there, she caught hold of him, and said:

"I'll tell papa."

"Oh no, you won't!" returned the prince.

"Yes, I will," she persisted. "What business had you to pull me down out of the water, and throw me to the bottom of the air? I never did you any harm."

"Pardon me. I did not mean to hurt you."

"I don't believe you have any brains, and that is a worse loss than your wretched gravity. I pity you."

The prince now saw that he had come upon the bewitched princess, and had already offended her. But before he could think what to say next, she burst out angrily, giving a stamp with her foot that would have sent her aloft again but for the hold she had of his arm:

"Put me up directly."

"Put you up where, you beauty?" asked the prince.

He had fallen in love with her almost already, for her anger made her more charming than any one else had ever beheld her; and, as far as he could see, which certainly was not far, she had not a single fault about her, except, of course, that she had not any gravity. No prince, however, would judge of a princess by weight. The loveliness of her foot he would hardly estimate by the depth of the impression it could make in mud.

"Put you up where, you beauty?" asked the prince.

"In the water, you stupid!" answered the princess.

"Come then," said the prince.

The condition of her dress increasing her usual difficulty in walking, compelled her to cling to him, and he could hardly persuade himself that he was not in a delightful dream, notwithstanding the torrent of musical abuse with which she overwhelmed him. The prince being therefore in no hurry, they came upon the lake at quite another part, where the bank was twenty-

"THE PRINCESS HAD JUST TIME TO GIVE ONE DELIGHTED SHRIEK
OF LAUGHTER BEFORE THE WATER CLOSED OVER THEM"

five feet high at least; and when they had reached the edge, he turned toward the princess and said:

"How am I to put you in?"

"That is your business," she answered, quite snappishly. "You took me out—put me in again."

"Very well," said the prince, and catching her up in his arms, he sprang with her from the rock. The princess had just time to give one delighted shriek of laughter before the water closed over them. When they came to the surface, she found that for a moment or two she could not even laugh, for she had gone down with such a rush that it was with difficulty she recovered her breath. The instant they reached the surface—

"How do you like falling in?" said the prince.

After some effort the princess panted out:

"Is that what you call *falling in?*"

"Yes," answered the prince, "I should think it a very tolerable specimen."

"It seemed to me like going up," rejoined she.

"My feeling was certainly one of elevation, too," the prince conceded.

The princess did not appear to understand him, for she retorted his question:

"How do *you* like falling in?" said the princess.

"Beyond everything," answered he, "for I have fallen in with the only perfect creature I ever saw."

"No more of that. I am tired of it," said the princess.

Perhaps she shared her father's aversion to punning.

"Don't you like falling in, then?" said the prince.

"It is the most delightful fun I ever had in my life," answered she. "I never fell before. I wish I could learn. To think I am the only person in my father's kingdom that can't fall!"

Here the poor princess looked almost sad.

"I shall be most happy to fall in with you any time you like," said the prince devotedly.

"Thank you. I don't know. Perhaps it would not be proper. But I don't care. At all events, as we have fallen in, let us have a swim together."

"With all my heart," responded the prince.

And away they went, swimming and diving and floating, until at last they heard cries along the shore, and saw lights glancing in all directions. It was now quite late, and there was no moon.

"I must go home," said the princess. "I am very sorry, for this is delightful."

"So am I," returned the prince. "But I am glad I haven't a home to go to—at least, I don't exactly know where it is."

"I wish I hadn't one, either," rejoined the princess, "it is so stupid! I have a great mind," she continued, "to play them all a trick. Why couldn't they leave me alone? They won't trust me in the lake for a single night! You see where that green light is burning? That is the window of my room. Now if you would just swim there with me very quietly, and when we are all but under the balcony, give me such a push—*up* you call it—as you did a little while ago, I should be able to catch hold of the balcony and get in at the window, and then they may look for me till to-morrow morning!"

"With more obedience than pleasure," said the prince gallantly, and away they swam very gently.

"Will you be in the lake to-morrow night?" the prince ventured to ask.

"To be sure I will. I don't think so. Perhaps," was the princess's somewhat strange answer.

But the prince was intelligent enough not to press her further, and merely whispered, as he gave her the parting lift, "Don't tell." The only answer the princess returned was a roguish look. She was already a yard above his head. The look seemed to say, "Never fear. It is too good fun to spoil that way."

So perfectly like other people had she been in the water, that even yet the prince could scarcely believe his eyes when he saw her ascend slowly, grasp the balcony, and disappear through the window. He turned, almost expecting to see her still by his side. But he was alone in the water. So he swam away quietly, and watched the lights roving about the shore for hours after the princess was safe in her chamber. As soon as they disappeared, he landed in search of his tunic and sword, and after some trouble, found them again. Then he made the best of his way round the lake to the other side. There the wood was wilder and the shore steeper—rising more immediately toward the mountains which surrounded the lake on all sides, and kept sending it messages of silvery streams from morning to night and all night long. He soon found a spot where he could see the green light in the princess's room, and where, even in the broad daylight, he would be in no danger of being discovered from the opposite shore. It was a sort of cave in the rock, where he provided himself a bed of withered leaves, and lay down too tired for hunger to keep him awake. All night long he dreamed that he was swimming with the princess.

X

Look at the Moon

Early the next morning the prince set out to look for something to eat, which he soon found at a forester's hut, where for many following days he was supplied with all that a brave prince could consider necessary. And having plenty to keep him alive for the present, he would not think of wants not yet in existence. Whenever Care intruded, this prince always bowed him out in the most princely manner.

When he returned from his breakfast to his watch-cave, he saw the princess already floating about in the lake, attended by the king and queen—whom he knew by their crowns—and a great company in lovely little boats, with canopies of all the colours of the rainbow, and flags and streamers of a great many more. It was a very bright day, and soon the prince, burned up with the heat, began to long for the cold water and the cool princess. But he had to endure till twilight, for the boats had provisions on board, and it was not till the sun went down that the gay party began to vanish. Boat after boat drew away to the shore, following that of the king and queen, till only one, apparently the princess's own boat, remained. But she did not want to go home even yet, and the prince thought he saw her order the boat to the shore without her. At all events it rowed away; and now, of all the radiant company, only one white speck remained. Then the prince began to sing. And this is what he sung:

"Lady fair,
  Swan-white,
Lift thine eyes,
  Banish night
By the might
  Of thine eyes.

"Snowy arms,
  Oars of snow,
  Oar her hither,
  Plashing low.
  Soft and slow,
  Oar her hither.

"Stream behind her
  O'er the lake,
  Radiant whiteness!
  In her wake
  Following, following, for her sake,
  Radiant whiteness!

"Cling about her,
  Waters blue;
  Part not from her,
  But renew
  Cold and true
  Kisses round her.

"Lap me round,
  Waters sad
  That have left her
  Make me glad,
  For ye had
  Kissed her ere ye left her."

Before he had finished his song, the princess was just under the place where he sat and looking up to find him. Her ears had led her truly.

"Would you like a fall, princess?" said the prince, looking down.

"Ah! there you are! Yes, if you please, prince," said the princess, looking up.

"How do you know I am a prince, princess?" said the prince.

"Because you are a very nice young man, prince," said the princess.

"Come up then, princess."

"Fetch me, prince."

The prince took off his scarf, then his sword belt, then his tunic, and tied them all together and let them down. But the line was far too short. He unwound his turban and added it to the rest, when it was all but long enough, and his purse completed it. The princess just managed to lay hold of the knot of money, and was beside him in a moment. This rock was much higher than the other, and the splash and the dive were tremendous. The princess was in ecstasies of delight, and their swim was delicious.

Night after night they met and swam about in the dark clear lake, where such was the prince's gladness that (whether the princess's way of looking at things affected him, or he was actually getting light-headed) he often fancied that he was swimming in the sky in-stead of the lake. But when he talked about being in heaven, the princess laughed at him dreadfully.

When the moon came, she brought them fresh pleasure. Everything looked strange and new in her light, with an old, withered, yet unfading newness. When the moon was nearly full, one of their great delights was to dive deep in the water, and then, turning round, look up through it at the great blot of light close above them, shimmering and trembling and wavering, spreading and contracting, seeming to melt away and again grow solid. Then they would shoot up through the blot, and lo! there was the moon, far off, clear and steady and cold, and very lovely at the bottom of a deeper and bluer lake than theirs, as the princess said.

The prince soon found out that while in the water the princess was very like other people. And besides this, she was not so forward in her questions or pert in her replies at sea as on shore. Neither did she laugh so much, and when she did laugh, it was more gently. She seemed altogether more modest and maidenly in the water than out of it. But when the prince, who had really fallen in love when he fell in the lake, began to talk to her about love, she always turned her head toward him and laughed. After a while she began to look puzzled, as if she were trying to understand what he

106

meant but could not—revealing a notion that he meant
something. But as soon as ever she left the lake, she
was so altered that the prince said to himself, "If I marry
her, I see no help for it: we must turn merman and mer-
maid, and go out to sea at once."

XI

Hiss!

The princess's pleasure in the lake had grown to a
passion, and she could scarcely bear to be out of it for an
hour. Imagine then her consternation when, diving
with the prince one night, a sudden suspicion seized her
that the lake was not so deep as it used to be. The
prince could not imagine what had happened. She
shot to the surface, and, without a word, swam at full
speed toward the higher side of the lake. He followed,
begging to know if she was ill, or what was the matter.
She never turned her head or took the smallest notice
of his question. Arrived at the shore, she coasted the
rocks with minute inspection, but she was not able to
come to a conclusion, for the moon was very small and
so she could not see well. She turned therefore and
swam home, without saying a word to explain her
conduct to the prince, of whose presence she seemed
no longer conscious. He withdrew to his cave in great
perplexity and distress.

Next day she made many observations, which, alas! strengthened her fears. She saw that the banks were too dry, and that the grass on the shore and the trailing plants on the rocks were withering away. She caused marks to be made along the borders, and examined them day by day in all directions of the wind, till at last the horrible idea became a certain fact—that the surface of the lake was slowly sinking.

The poor princess nearly went out of the little mind she had. It was awful to her to see the lake, which she loved more than any living thing, lie dying before her eyes. It sank away, slowly vanishing. The tops of rocks that had never been seen till now began to appear far down in the clear water. Before long they were dry in the sun. It was fearful to think of the mud that would soon lie there baking and festering, full of lovely creatures dying and ugly creatures coming to life, like the unmaking of a world. And how hot the sun would be without any lake! She could not bear to swim in it any more, and began to pine away. Her life seemed bound up with it, and ever as the lake sank, she pined. People said she would not live an hour after the lake was gone.

But she never cried.

Proclamation was made to all the kingdom that whosoever should discover the cause of the lake's decrease would be rewarded after a princely fashion.

Hum-Drum and Kopy-Keck applied themselves to their physics and metaphysics, but in vain. Not even they could suggest a cause.

Now the fact was that the old princess was at the root of the mischief. When she heard that her niece found more pleasure in the water than any one else had out of it, she went into a rage and cursed herself for her want of foresight.

"But," said she, "I will soon set all right. The king and the people shall die of thirst; their brains shall boil and frizzle in their skulls before I will lose my revenge."

And she laughed a ferocious laugh, that made the hairs on the back of her black cat stand erect with terror.

Then she went to an old chest in the room, and opening it, took out what looked like a piece of dried seaweed. This she threw into a tub of water. Then she threw some powder into the water and stirred it with her bare arm, muttering over it words of hideous sound and yet more hideous import. Then she set the tub aside, and took from the chest a huge bunch of a hundred rusty keys that clattered in her shaking hands. Then she sat down and proceeded to oil them all. Before she had finished, out from the tub, the water of which had kept on a slow motion ever since she had ceased stirring it, came the head and half the body of a huge gray snake.

But the witch did not look round. It grew out of the tub, waving itself backward and forward with a slow horizontal motion till it reached the princess, when it laid its head upon her shoulder and gave a low hiss in her ear. She started—but with joy, and seeing the head resting on her shoulder drew it toward her and kissed it. Then she drew it all out of the tub, and wound it round her body. It was one of those dreadful creatures which few have ever beheld—the White Snakes of Darkness.

Then she took the keys and went down to her cellar, and as she unlocked the door she said to herself:

"This *is* worth living for!"

Locking the door behind her, she descended a few steps into the cellar, and crossing it, unlocked another door into a dark, narrow passage. She locked this also behind her, and descended a few more steps. If any one had followed the witch-princess, he would have heard her unlock exactly one hundred doors and descend a few steps after unlocking each. When she had unlocked the last, she entered a vast cave, the roof of which was supported by huge natural pillars of rock. Now this roof was the under side of the bottom of the lake.

She then untwined the snake from her body, and held it by the tail high above her. The hideous creature stretched up its head toward the roof of the cavern, which it was just able to reach. It then began to move its head backward and forward, with a slow oscillating motion, as if looking for something. At the same moment the witch began to walk round and round the cavern, coming nearer to the centre every circuit; while the head of the snake described the same path over the roof that she did over the floor, for she kept holding it up. And still it kept slowly oscillating. Round and round the cavern they went, ever lessening the circuit, till at last the snake made a sudden dart, and clung to the roof with its mouth.

"That's right, my beauty!" cried the princess; "drain it dry."

She let it go, left it hanging, and sat down on a great stone, with her black cat, which had followed her all round the cave, by her side. Then she began to knit and mutter awful words. The snake hung like a huge leech, sucking at the stone; the cat stood with his back arched, and his tail like a piece of cable, looking up at the snake; and the old woman sat and knitted and muttered. Seven days and seven nights they remained thus; when suddenly the serpent dropped from the roof as if exhausted, and shrivelled up till it was again like a piece of dried seaweed. The witch started to her feet, picked it up, put it in her pocket, and looked up at the roof. One drop of water was trembling on the spot where the snake had been sucking. As soon as she saw that, she turned and fled, followed by her cat. Shutting the door in a terrible hurry, she locked it, and having muttered some frightful words, sped to the next, which also she locked and muttered over; and so with all the hundred doors, till she arrived in her own cellar. Then she sat down on the floor ready to faint, but listening with malicious delight to the rushing of the water, which she could hear distinctly through all the hundred doors.

But this was not enough. Now that she had tasted revenge, she lost her patience. Without further measures, the lake would be too long in disappearing. So the next night, with the last shred of the dying old moon rising, she took some of the water in which she had revived the snake, put it in a bottle, and set out, accompanied by her cat. Before morning she had made the entire circuit of the lake, muttering fearful words as she crossed every stream and casting into it some of the water out of her bottle. When she had finished the circuit, she muttered yet again and flung a handful of water toward the moon. Thereupon every spring in the country ceased to throb and bubble, dying away like the pulse of a dying man. The next day there was no sound of falling water to be heard along the borders of the lake. The very courses were dry, and the mountains showed no silvery streams down their dark sides. And not alone had the fountains of Mother Earth ceased to flow, for all the babies throughout the country were crying dreadfully—only without tears.

XII

Where Is the Prince?

Never since the night when the princess left him so abruptly had the prince had a single interview with her. He had seen her once or twice in the lake, but as far as he could discover, she had not been in it any more at night. He had sat and sung and looked in vain for his Nereid, while she, like a true Nereid, was wasting away with her lake, sinking as it sank, withering as it dried. When at length he discovered the change that was taking place in the level of the water, he was in great alarm and perplexity. He could not tell whether the lake was dying because the lady had forsaken it, or whether the lady would not come because the lake had begun to sink. But he resolved to know so much at least.

He disguised himself, and going to the palace, requested to see the lord chamberlain. His appearance at once gained his request, and the lord chamberlain, being a man of some insight, perceived that there was more in the prince's solicitation than met the ear. He felt likewise that no one could tell whence a solution of the present difficulties might arise. So he granted the

113

prince's prayer to be made shoeblack to the princess. It was rather cunning in the prince to request such an easy post, for the princess could not possibly soil as many shoes as other princesses.

He soon learned all that could be told about the princess. He went nearly distracted; but after roaming about the lake for days, and diving in every depth that remained, all that he could do was to put an extra polish on the dainty pair of boots that was never called for.

For the princess kept her room, with the curtains drawn to shut out the dying lake, but could not shut it out of her mind for a moment. It haunted her imagination so that she felt as if the lake were her soul, drying up within her, first to mud, then to madness and death. She thus brooded over the change, with all its dreadful accompaniments, till she was nearly distracted. As for the prince, she had forgotten him. However much she had enjoyed his company in the water, she did not care for him without it. But she seemed to have forgotten her father and mother too.

The lake went on sinking. Small slimy spots began to appear, which glittered steadily amidst the changeful shine of the water. These grew to broad patches of mud, which widened and spread, with rocks here and there, and floundering fishes and crawling eels swarming. The people went everywhere catching these, and looking for anything that might have dropped from the royal boats.

At length the lake was all but gone, only a few of the deepest pools remaining unexhausted.

It happened one day that a party of youngsters found themselves on the brink of one of these pools in the very centre of the lake. It was a rocky basin of considerable depth. Looking in, they saw at the bottom something that shone yellow in the sun. A little boy jumped in and dived for it. It was a plate of gold covered with writing. They carried it to the king.

On one side of it stood these words:

> "Death alone from death can save.
> Love is death, and so is brave.
> Love can fill the deepest grave.
> Love loves on beneath the wave."

Now this was enigmatical enough to the king and courtiers. But the reverse of the plate explained it a little. Its writing amounted to this:

"If the lake should disappear, they must find the hole through which the water ran. But it would be useless to try to stop it by any ordinary means. There was but one effectual mode. The body of a living man could alone staunch the flow. The man must give himself of his own will; and the lake must take his life as it filled. Otherwise the offering would be of no avail. If the nation could not provide one hero, it was time it should perish."

XIII

Here I Am!

This was a very disheartening revelation to the king —not that he was unwilling to sacrifice a subject, but that he was hopeless of finding a man willing to sacrifice himself. No time was to be lost, however, for the princess was lying motionless on her bed, and taking no nourishment but lake water, which was now none of the best. Therefore the king caused the contents of the wonderful plate of gold to be published throughout the country.

No one, however, came forward.

The prince, having gone several days' journey into the forest, to consult a hermit whom he had met there on his way to Lagobel, knew nothing of the oracle till his return.

When he had acquainted himself with all the particulars, he sat down and thought:

"She will die if I don't do it, and life would be nothing to me without her; so I shall lose nothing by doing it. And life will be as pleasant to her as ever, for she will soon forget me. And there will be so much more beauty and happiness in the world! To be sure, I shall not see it." (Here the poor prince gave a sigh.) "How lovely the lake will be in the moonlight, with that glorious creature sporting in it like a wild goddess! It is rather hard to be drowned by inches, though. Let me see—that will be seventy inches of me to drown." (Here he tried to laugh, but could not.) "The longer the better, however," he resumed, "for can I not bargain that the princess shall be beside me all the time? So I shall see her once more, kiss her perhaps—who knows? And die looking in her eyes. It will be no death. At least, I shall not feel it. And to see the lake filling for the beauty again! All right! I am ready."

He kissed the princess's boot, laid it down, and hurried to the king's apartment. But feeling, as he went, that anything sentimental would be disagreeable, he resolved to carry off the whole affair with nonchalance. So he knocked at the door of the king's counting-house, where it was all but a capital crime to disturb him.

When the king heard the knock he started up and opened the door in a rage. Seeing only the shoeblack, he drew his sword. This, I am sorry to say, was his usual mode of asserting his regality when he thought his dignity was in danger. But the prince was not in the least alarmed.

"Please, your Majesty, I'm your butler," said he.

"My butler! you lying rascal! What do you mean?"

"I mean I will cork your big bottle."

"Is the fellow mad?" bawled the king, raising the point of his sword.

"I will put the stopper—plug—what you call it, in your leaky lake, grand monarch," said the prince.

The king was in such a rage that before he could speak he had time to cool, and to reflect that it would be great waste to kill the only man who was willing to be useful in the present emergency, seeing that in the end the insolent fellow would be as dead as if he had died by his Majesty's own hand.

"Oh!" said he at last, putting up his sword with difficulty, it was so long; "I am obliged to you, you young fool! Take a glass of wine?"

"No, thank you," replied the prince.

"Very well," said the king. "Would you like to run and see your parents before you make your experiment?"

"No, thank you," said the prince.

"Then we will go and look for the hole at once," said his Majesty, and proceeded to call some attendants.

"Stop, please your Majesty, I have a condition to make," interposed the prince.

"What!" exclaimed the king, "a condition! and with me! How dare you?"

"As you please," returned the prince coolly, "I wish your Majesty a good morning."

"You wretch! I will have you put in a sack and stuck in the hole."

"Very well, your Majesty," replied the prince, becoming a little more respectful lest the wrath of the king should deprive him of the pleasure of dying for the princess. "But what good will that do your Majesty? Please to remember that the oracle says the victim must offer himself."

"Well, you *have* offered yourself," retorted the king.

"Yes, upon one condition."

"Condition again!" roared the king, once more drawing his sword. "Begone! Somebody else will be glad enough to take the honour off your shoulders."

"Your Majesty knows it will not be easy to get another to take my place."

"Well, what is your condition?" growled the king, feeling that the prince was right.

"Only this," replied the prince; "that, as I must on no account die before I am fairly drowned, and the waiting will be rather wearisome, the princess, your daughter, shall go with me, feed me with her own hands, and look at me now and then to comfort me, for you must confess it *is* rather hard. As soon as the water is up to my eyes, she may go and be happy, and forget her poor shoeblack."

Here the prince's voice faltered, and he very nearly grew sentimental in spite of his resolution.

119

"Why didn't you tell me before what your condition was? Such a fuss about nothing!" exclaimed the king.

"Do you grant it?" persisted the prince.

"Of course I do," replied the king.

"Very well. I am ready."

"Go and have some dinner, then, while I set my people to find the place."

The king ordered out his guards, and gave directions to the officers to find the hole in the lake at once. So the bed of the lake was marked out in divisions and thoroughly examined, and in an hour or so the hole was discovered. It was in the middle of a stone, near the centre of the lake, in the very pool where the golden plate had been found. It was a three-cornered hole of no great size. There was water all round the stone, but very little was flowing through the hole.

XIV

This Is Very Kind of You

The prince went to dress for the occasion, for he was resolved to die like a prince.

When the princess heard that a man had offered to die for her, she was so transported that she jumped off the bed, feeble as she was, and danced about the room for joy. She did not care who the man was; that was nothing to her. The hole wanted stopping, and if only a man would do, why, take one. In an hour or two more everything was ready. Her maid dressed her in haste, and they carried her to the side of the lake. When she saw it she shrieked, and covered her face with her hands. They bore her across to the stone, where they had already placed a little boat for her. The water was not deep enough to float in, but they hoped it would be before long. They laid her on cushions, placed in the boat wines and fruits and other nice things, and stretched a canopy over all.

In a few minutes the prince appeared. The princess recognized him at once, but did not think it worth while to acknowledge him.

"Here I am," said the prince. "Put me in."

"They told me it was a shoeblack," said the princess.

"So I am," said the prince. "I blacked your little boots three times a day because they were all I could get of you. Put me in."

The courtiers did not resent his bluntness, except by saying to each other that he was taking it out in impudence.

But how was he to be put in? The golden plate contained no instructions on this point. The prince looked at the hole, and saw but one way. He put both his legs into it, sitting on the stone, and, stooping forward, covered the corner that remained open with his

two hands.   In this uncomfortable position he resolved
to abide his fate, and turning to the people said:

"Now you can go."

The king had already gone home to dinner.

"Now you can go," repeated the princess after him
like a parrot.

The people obeyed her and went.

Presently a little wave flowed over the stone and
wetted one of the prince's knees.   But he did not mind it
much.   He began to sing, and the song he sang was this:

"As a world that has no well,
 Darkly bright in forest dell;
 As a world without the gleam
 Of the downward-going stream;
 As a world without the glance
 Of the ocean's fair-expanse;
 As a world where never rain
 Glittered on the sunny plain;—
 Such, my heart, thy world would be
 If no love did flow in thee.

"As a world without the sound
 Of the rivulets underground;
 Or the bubbling of the spring
 Out of darkness wandering;
 Or the mighty rush and flowing
 Of the river's downward going;

122

Or the music showers that drop
On the outspread beech's top;
Or the ocean's mighty voice,
When his lifted waves rejoice;—
Such, my soul, thy world would be
If no love did sing in thee.

"Lady, keep thy world's delight,
Keep the waters in thy sight.
Love hath made me strong to go,
For thy sake, to realms below,
Where the water's shine and hum
Through the darkness never come.
Let, I pray, one thought of me
Spring, a little well, in thee;
Lest thy loveless soul be found
Like a dry and thirsty ground.'

"Sing again, prince. It makes it less tedious," said the princess.

But the prince was too much overcome to sing any more, and a long pause followed.

"This is very kind of you, prince," said the princess at last, quite coolly, as she lay in the boat with her eyes shut.

"I am sorry I can't return the compliment," thought the prince, "but you are worth dying for, after all."

Again a wavelet, and another, and another, flowed

over the stone and wetted both the prince's knees, but he did not speak or move. Two—three—four hours passed in this way, the princess apparently asleep and the prince very patient. But he was much disappointed in his position, for he had none of the consolation he had hoped for.

At last he could bear it no longer.

"Princess!" said he.

But at the moment up started the princess, crying: "I'm afloat! I'm afloat!"

And the little boat bumped against the stone.

"Princess!" repeated the prince, encouraged by seeing her wide awake and looking eagerly at the water.

"Well?" said she, without looking round.

"Your papa promised that you should look at me, and you haven't looked at me once."

"Did he? Then I suppose I must. But I am so sleepy!"

"Sleep, then, darling, and don't mind me," said the poor prince.

"Really, you are very good," replied the princess. "I think I will go to sleep again."

"Just give me a glass of wine and a biscuit first," said the prince, very humbly.

"With all my heart," said the princess, and yawned as she said it.

She got the wine and the biscuit, however, and leaning over the side of the boat toward him, was compelled to look at him.

"Why, prince," she said, "you don't look well! Are you sure you don't mind it?"

"Not a bit," answered he, feeling very faint indeed. "Only I shall die before it is of any use to you, unless I have something to eat."

"There, then," said she, holding out the wine to him.

"Ah! you must feed me. I dare not move my hands. The water would run away directly."

"Good gracious!" said the princess; and she began at once to feed him with bits of biscuit and sips of wine.

As she fed him he contrived to kiss the tips of her fingers now and then. She did not seem to mind it, one way or the other. But the prince felt better.

"Now, for your own sake, princess," said he, "I cannot let you go to sleep. You must sit and look at me, else I shall not be able to keep up."

"Well, I will do anything to oblige you," answered she, with condescension; and, sitting down, she did look at him, and kept looking at him with wonderful steadiness, considering all things.

The sun went down, and the moon rose, and, gush after gush, the waters were rising up the prince's body. They were up to his waist now.

"Why can't we go and have a swim?" said the princess. "There seems to be water enough just about here."

"I shall never swim more," said the prince.

"Oh, I forgot," said the princess, and was silent.

So the water grew and grew, and rose up and up on the prince. And the princess sat and looked at him. She fed him now and then. The night wore on. The waters rose and rose. The moon rose likewise higher and higher, and shone full on the face of the dying prince. The water was up to his neck.

"Will you kiss me, princess?" said he feebly. The nonchalance was all gone now.

"Yes, I will," answered the princess, and kissed him with a long, sweet, cold kiss.

"Now," said he, with a sigh of content, "I die happy."

He did not speak again. The princess gave him some wine for the last time: he was past eating. Then she sat down again, and looked at him. The water rose and rose. It touched his chin. It touched his lower lip. It touched between his lips. He shut them hard to keep it out. The princess began to feel strange. It touched his upper lip. He breathed through his nostrils. The princess looked wild. It covered his nostrils. Her eyes looked scared and shone strange in the moonlight. His head fell back; the water closed over it, and the bubbles of his last breath bubbled up through the water. The princess gave a shriek and sprang into the lake.

She laid hold first of one leg and then of the other, and pulled and tugged, but she could not move either. She stopped to take breath, and that made her think that he could not get any breath. She was frantic. She got hold of him and held his head above the water, which was possible now his hands were no longer on the hole. But it was of no use, for he was past breathing.

Love and water brought back all her strength. She got under the water, and pulled and pulled with her whole might, till at last she got one leg out. The other easily followed. How she got him into the boat she never could tell; but when she did, she fainted away. Coming to herself, she seized the oars, kept herself steady as best she could, and rowed and rowed, though she had never rowed before. Round rocks and over shallows and through mud she rowed, till she got to the landing-stairs of the palace. By this time her people were on the shore, for they had heard her shriek. She made them carry the prince to her own room, and lay him in her bed, and light a fire, and send for the doctors.

"But the lake, your highness!" said the chamberlain who, roused by the noise, came in in his nightcap.

"Go and drown yourself in it!" she said.

This was the last rudeness of which the princess was

ever guilty, and one must allow that she had good cause to feel provoked with the lord chamberlain.

Had it been the king himself, he would have fared no better. But both he and the queen were fast asleep. And the chamberlain went back to his bed. Somehow, the doctors never came. So the princess and her old nurse were left with the prince. But the old nurse was a wise woman, and knew what to do.

They tried everything for a long time without success. The princess was nearly distracted between hope and fear, but she tried on and on, one thing after another, and everything over and over again.

At last, when they had all but given it up, just as the sun rose the prince opened his eyes.

XV

Look at the Rain!

The princess burst into a passion of tears and *fell* on the floor. There she lay for an hour, and her tears never ceased. All the pent-up crying of her life was spent now. And a rain came on, such as had never been seen in that country. The sun shone all the time, and the great drops, which fell straight to the earth, shone likewise. The palace was in the heart of a rainbow. It was a rain of rubies, and sapphires, and emeralds, and topazes. The torrents poured from the mountains like molten gold; and if it had not been for its subterraneous outlet, the lake would have overflowed and inundated the country. It was full from shore to shore.

But the princess did not heed the lake. She lay on the floor and wept. And this rain within doors was far more wonderful than the rain out of doors, for when it abated a little, and she proceeded to rise, she found to her astonishment that she could not. At length, after many efforts, she succeeded in getting upon her feet. But she tumbled down again directly. Hearing her fall, her old nurse uttered a yell of delight, and ran to her screaming:

"My darling child! she's found her gravity!"

"Oh, that's it, is it?" said the princess, rubbing her shoulder and her knee alternately. "I consider it very unpleasant. I feel as if I should be crushed to pieces."

"Hurrah!" cried the prince from the bed. "If you've come round, princess, so have I. How's the lake?"

"Brimful," answered the nurse.

"Then we're all happy."

"That we are indeed!" answered the princess, sobbing.

And there was rejoicing all over the country that rainy day. Even the babies forgot their past troubles, and danced and crowed amazingly. And the king told stories and the queen listened to them. And he divided the money in his box, and she the honey in her pot, among all the children. And there was such jubilation as was never heard of before.

Of course the prince and princess were betrothed at once. But the princess had to learn to walk before they could be married with any propriety. And this was not so easy at her time of life, for she could walk no more than a baby. She was always falling down and hurting herself.

"Is this the gravity you used to make so much of?" said she one day to the prince, as he raised her from the floor. "For my part, I was a great deal more comfortable without it."

"No, no, that's not it. This is it," replied the prince, as he took her up and carried her about like a baby, kissing her all the time. "This is gravity."

"That's better," said she. "I don't mind that so much."

And she smiled the sweetest, loveliest smile in the prince's face. And she gave him one little kiss in return for all his; and he thought them overpaid, for he was beside himself with delight. I fear she complained of her gravity more than once after this, notwithstanding.

It was a long time before she got reconciled to walking. But the pain of learning it was quite counterbalanced by two things, either of which would have been sufficient consolation. The first was that the prince himself was her teacher, and the second, that she could tumble into the lake as often as she pleased. Still, she preferred to have the prince jump in with her, and the splash they made before was nothing to the splash they made now. The lake never sank again. In process of time it wore the roof of the cavern quite through, and was twice as deep as before.

The only revenge the princess took upon her aunt was to tread pretty hard on her gouty toe the next time she saw her. But she was sorry for it the very next day, when she heard that the water had undermined her house, and that it had fallen in the night, burying her in its ruins, whence no one ever ventured to dig up her body. There she lies to this day.

So the prince and princess lived and were happy; and had crowns of gold, and clothes of cloth, and shoes of leather, and children of boys and girls, not one of whom was ever known, on the most critical occasion, to lose the smallest atom of his or her due proportion of gravity.

BEAUTY AND THE BEAST

THERE was once a very rich merchant who had
six children, three boys and three girls. As he
was himself a man of great sense, he spared no
expense for their education, but provided them with all
sorts of masters for their improvement. The three
daughters were all handsome, but particularly the
youngest; indeed she was so very beautiful that in her
childhood every one called her the Little Beauty, and
being still the same when she was grown up, nobody
called her by any other name, which made her sisters
very jealous of her. This youngest daughter was not
only more handsome than her sisters, but was also
better tempered. The two eldest were vain of being

132

rich, and spoke with pride to those they thought below them. They gave themselves a thousand airs, and would not visit other merchants' daughters, nor would they indeed be seen with any but persons of quality. They went every day to balls, plays, and public walks, and always made game of their youngest sister for spending her time in reading or other useful employments. As it was well known that these young ladies would have large fortunes, many great merchants wished to get them for wives; but the two eldest always answered that, for their parts, they had no thoughts of marrying any one below a duke, or an earl at least. Beauty had quite as many offers as her sisters, but she always answered with the greatest civility that she was much obliged to her lovers but would rather live some years longer with her father, as she thought herself too young to marry.

It happened that by some unlucky accident the merchant suddenly lost all his fortune, and had nothing left but a small cottage in the country. Upon this, he said to his daughters while the tears ran down his cheeks all the time, " My children, we must now go and dwell in the cottage and try to get a living by labour, for we have no other means of support." The two eldest replied that, for their parts, they did not know how to work and would not leave town for they had lovers enough who would be glad to marry them though they had no longer any fortune. But in this they were mistaken, for when the lovers heard what had happened, they said, "The girls were so proud and ill-tempered that all we wanted was their fortune; we are not sorry at all to see their pride brought down. Let them give themselves airs to their cows and sheep." But everybody pitied poor Beauty because she was so sweet-tempered and kind to all that knew her, and several gentlemen offered to marry her, though she had not a penny; but Beauty still refused, and said she could not think of leaving her poor father in this trouble and would go and help him in his labours in the country. At first Beauty could not help sometimes crying in secret for the hardships she was now obliged to suffer; but in a very short time she said to herself, "All the crying in the world will do me no good, so I will try to be happy without a fortune."

When they had removed to their cottage, the merchant and his three sons employed themselves in ploughing and sowing the fields and working in the garden. Beauty also did her part, for she got up by four o'clock every morning, lighted the fires, cleaned the house, and got the breakfast for the whole family. At first she found all this very hard; but she soon grew quite used to it, and thought it no hardship at all; and indeed the work greatly amended her health. When she had done, she used to amuse herself with reading, playing on her music, or singing while she spun. But her two sisters

134

were at a loss what to do to pass the time away: they had their breakfast in bed, and did not rise till ten o'clock. Then they commonly walked out, but always found themselves very soon tired, when they would often sit down under a shady tree, and grieve for the loss of their carriage and fine clothes, and say to each other, "What a mean-spirited, poor, stupid creature our young sister is to be so content with our low way of life!" But their father thought in quite another way: he admired the patience of this sweet young creature; for her sisters not only left her to do the whole work of the house, but made game of her every moment.

After they had lived in this manner about a year, the merchant received a letter, which informed him that one of the richest ships which he thought was lost had just come into port. This news made the two eldest sisters almost mad with joy, for they thought they should now leave the cottage and have all their finery again. When they found that their father must take a journey to the ship, the two eldest begged he would not fail to bring them back some new gowns, caps, rings, and all sorts of trinkets. But Beauty asked for nothing, for she thought in herself that all the ship was worth would hardly buy everything her sisters wished for. "Beauty," said the merchant, "how comes it about that you ask for nothing; what can I bring you, my child?" "Since you are so kind as to think of me, dear father," she

135

answered, "I should be glad if you would bring me a rose, for we have none in our garden." Now Beauty did not indeed wish for a rose nor anything else, but she only said this that she might not affront her sisters, or else they would have said she wanted her father to praise her for not asking him for anything. The merchant took his leave of them and set out on his journey; but when he got to the ship some persons went to law with him about the cargo, and after a deal of trouble he came back to his cottage as poor as he had gone away. When he was within thirty miles of his home and thinking of the joy he should have in again meeting his children, his road lay through a thick forest and he quite lost himself. It rained and snowed very hard and, besides, the wind was so high as to throw him twice from his horse. Night came on, and he thought to be sure he should die of cold and hunger or be torn to pieces by the wolves that he heard howling round him. All at once he now cast his eyes toward a long row of trees and saw a light at the end of them, but it seemed a great way off. He made the best of his way toward it, and found that it came from a fine palace, lighted all over. He walked faster, soon reached the gates, which he opened, and was very much surprised that he did not see a single person or creature in any of the yards. His horse had followed him, and finding a stable with the door open, went into it at once; and here the poor beast, being nearly starved, helped himself to a good meal of oats and hay. His master then tied him up and walked toward the house, which he entered, but still without seeing a living creature. He went on to a large hall, where he found a good fire and a table covered with some very nice dishes, but only one plate with a knife and fork. As the snow and rain had wetted him to the skin, he went up to the fire to dry himself. "I hope," said he, "the master of the house or his servants will excuse me, for to be sure it will not be long now before I see them." He waited a good time, but still nobody came; at last the clock struck eleven, and the merchant, being quite faint for the want of food, helped himself to a chicken, which he made but two mouthfuls of, and then to a few glasses of wine, yet all the time trembling with fear. He sat till the clock struck twelve, but did not see a single creature. He now took courage and began to think of looking a little more about him; so he opened a door at the end of the hall, and went through it into a very grand room, in which there was a fine bed; and as he was quite weak and tired, he shut the door, took off his clothes, and got into it.

It was ten o'clock in the morning before he thought of getting up, when he was amazed to see a handsome new suit of clothes laid ready for him instead of his own, which he had spoiled. "To be sure," said he to himself, "this place belongs to some good fairy who has taken pity on my ill luck." He looked out of the window, and, instead of snow, he saw the most charming arbours covered with all kinds of flowers. He returned to the hall where he had supped, and found a breakfast table, with some chocolate ready for him. "Indeed, my good fairy," said the merchant aloud, "I am vastly obliged to you for your kind care of me." He then made a hearty breakfast, took his hat, and was going to the stable to pay his horse a visit, but as he passed under one of the arbours, which was loaded with roses, he thought of what Beauty had asked him to bring back to her, and so he took a bunch of roses to carry home. At the same moment he heard a most shocking noise, and saw such a frightful beast coming toward him that he was ready to drop with fear. "Ungrateful man!" said the beast in a terrible voice, "I have saved your life by letting you into my palace, and in return you steal my roses, which I value more than anything else that belongs to me. But you shall make amends for your fault with your life. You shall die in a quarter of an hour." The merchant fell on his knees to the beast, and, clasping his hands, said, "My lord, I humbly beg your pardon. I did not think it would offend you to gather a rose for one of my daughters who wished to have one." "I am not a lord, but a beast," replied the monster; "I do not like false compliments, but that people should say what they think, so do not fancy that you can coax me by any such ways. You tell me that you have daughters; now I will pardon you if one of them will agree to come and die instead of you. Go, and if your daughters should refuse, promise me that you yourself will return in three months."

The tender-hearted merchant had no thought of letting any one of his daughters die instead of him, but he knew that if he seemed to accept the beast's terms, he should at least have the pleasure of seeing them once again. So he gave the beast his promise, and the beast told him he might then set off as soon as he liked. "But," said the beast, "I do not wish you to go back empty-handed. Go to the room you slept in, and you will find a chest there; fill it with just what you like best, and I will get it taken to your own house for you." When the beast had said this, he went away, and the good merchant said to himself, "If I must die, yet I shall now have the comfort of leaving my children some riches." He returned to the room he had slept in, and found a great many pieces of gold. He filled the chest with them to the very brim, locked it, and mounting his horse, left the palace as sorry as he had been glad when he first found it. The horse took a path across the forest of his own accord, and in a few hours they reached the merchant's house. His children came running round him as he got off his horse; but the merchant, instead of kissing them with joy, could not help crying as he looked at them. He held in his hand the bunch of roses, which he gave to Beauty, saying: "Take these roses, Beauty, but little do you think how dear they have cost your poor father," and then he gave them an account of all that he had seen or heard in the palace of the beast. The two eldest sisters now began to shed tears, and to lay the blame upon Beauty, who they said would be the cause of her father's death. "See," said they, "what happens from the pride of the little wretch? Why did not she ask for fine things as we did? But, to be sure, miss must not be like other people; and though she will be the cause of her father's death, yet she does not shed a tear." "It would be of no use," replied Beauty, "to weep for the death of my father, for he shall not die now. As the beast will accept one of his daughters, I will give myself up to him, and think myself happy in being able at once to save his life and prove my love for the best of fathers." "No, sister," said the three brothers, "you shall not die; we will go in search for this monster, and either he or we will perish." "Do not hope to kill him," said the merchant, "for his power is far too great for you to be able to do any such thing. I am charmed with the kindness of Beauty, but I will not suffer her life to be lost. I myself am old, and cannot expect to live much longer, so I shall but give up a few years of my life, and shall only grieve for the sake of my children." "Never, father," cried Beauty,

140

"shall you go to the palace without me, for you cannot hinder my going after you. Though young, I am not over fond of life, and I would much rather be eaten up by the monster than die of the grief your loss would give me." The merchant tried in vain to reason with Beauty, for she would go; which, in truth, made her two sisters glad, for they were jealous of her because everybody loved her.

The merchant was so grieved at the thoughts of losing his child that he never once thought of the chest filled with gold; but at night, to his great surprise, he found it standing by his bedside. He said nothing about his riches to his eldest daughters, for he knew very well it would at once make them want to return to town; but he told Beauty his secret, and she then said, that while he was away, two gentlemen had been on a visit to their cottage, who had fallen in love with her two sisters. She then begged her father to marry them without delay; for she was so sweet-tempered that she loved them for all they had used her so ill, and forgave them with all her heart. When the three months were past the merchant and Beauty got ready to set out for the palace of the beast. Upon this, the two sisters rubbed their eyes with an onion, to make believe they shed a great many tears, but both the merchant and his sons cried in earnest. There was only Beauty who did not, for she thought that this would only make the matter worse. They reached the palace in a very few hours, and the horse, without bidding, went into the same stable as before. The merchant and Beauty walked toward the large hall, where they found a table covered with every dainty, and two plates laid ready. The merchant had very little appetite; but Beauty, that she might the better hide her grief, placed herself at the table and helped her father; she then began herself to eat, and thought all the time that to be sure the beast had a mind to fatten her before he eat her up, as he had got such good cheer for her. When they had done their supper they heard a great noise, and the good old man began to bid his poor child farewell, for he knew it was the beast coming to them. When Beauty first saw his frightful form, she could not help being afraid, but she tried to hide her fear as much as she could. The beast asked her if she had come quite of her own accord, and though she was now still more afraid than before, she made shift to say, "Y-e-s." "You are a good girl, and I think myself very much obliged to you." He then turned toward her father, and said to him, "Good man, you may leave my palace to-morrow morning, and take care never to come back to it again. Good-night, Beauty." "Good-night, beast," said she, and then the monster went out of the room.

"Ah! my dear child," said the merchant, kissing his daughter, "I am half dead already at the thoughts of leaving you with this dreadful beast; you had better go back, and let me stay in your place." "No," said Beauty boldly, "I will never agree to that; you must go home to-morrow morning." Then they wished each other good-night, and went to bed, both of them thinking they should not be able to close their eyes; but as soon as ever they had laid down, they fell into a deep sleep and did not wake till morning. Beauty dreamed that a lady came up to her, who said, "I am very much pleased, Beauty, with the goodness you have shown in being willing to give your life to save that of your father, and it shall not go without a reward." As soon as Beauty awoke, she told her father this dream, but though it gave him some comfort, he could not take leave of his darling child without shedding many tears. When the merchant got out of sight Beauty sat down in the large hall and began to cry also; yet she had a great deal of courage, and so she soon resolved not to make her sad case still worse by sorrow, which she knew could not be of any use to her, but to wait as well as she could till night, when she thought the beast would not fail to come and eat her up. She walked about to take a view of all the palace, and the beauty of every part of it much charmed her.

But what was her surprise when she came to a door on which was written, *Beauty's room!* She opened it in haste, and her eyes were all at once dazzled at the

143

grandeur of the inside of the room. What made her wonder more than all the rest was a large library filled with books, a harpsichord, and many other pieces of music. "The beast takes care I shall not be at a loss how to amuse myself," said she. She then thought that it was not likely such things would have been got ready for her if she had but one day to live, and began to hope all would not turn out so bad as she and her father had feared. She opened the library, and saw these verses written in letters of gold on the back of one of the books:

"Beauteous lady, dry your tears,
　Here's no cause for sighs or fears;
Command as freely as you may,
　Enjoyment still shall mark your sway."

"Alas!" said she, sighing, "there is nothing I so much desire as to see my poor father and to know what he is doing at this moment." She said this to herself; but just then by chance she cast her eyes on a looking-glass that stood near her, and in the glass she saw her home, and her father riding up to the cottage in the deepest sorrow. Her sisters came out to meet him, but for all they tried to look sorry it was easy to see that in their hearts they were very glad. In a short time all this picture went away out of the glass, but Beauty began to

think that the beast was very kind to her and that she
had no need to be afraid of him. About the middle of
the day she found a table laid ready for her, and a
sweet concert of music played all the time she was eating
her dinner without her seeing a single creature. But at
supper, when she was going to seat herself at table, she
heard the noise of the beast, and could not help trembling with fear. "Beauty," said he, "will you give me
leave to see you sup?" "That is as you please," answered she, very much afraid. "Not in the least," said
the beast; "you alone command in this place. If you
should not like my company you need only to say so,
and I will leave you that moment. But tell me, Beauty,
do you not think me very ugly?" "Why, yes," said
she, "for I cannot tell a story, but then I think you are
very good." "You are right," replied the beast; "and,
besides being ugly, I am also very stupid; I know very
well enough that I am but a beast."

"I should think you cannot be very stupid," said
Beauty, "if you yourself know this." "Pray do not let
me hinder you from eating," said he, "and be sure you
do not want for anything, for all you see is yours, and I
shall be vastly grieved if you are not happy." "You
are very kind," said Beauty, "I must needs own that I
think very well of your good-nature, and then I almost
forget how ugly you are." "Yes, yes, I hope I am
good-tempered," said he, "but still I am a monster."

"There are many men who are worse monsters than you are," replied Beauty, "and I am better pleased with you in that form, though it is so ugly, than with those who carry wicked hearts under the form of a man." "If I had any sense," said the beast, "I would thank you for what you have said, but I am too stupid to say anything that would give you pleasure." Beauty ate her supper with a very good appetite, and almost lost all her dread of the monster; but she was ready to sink with fright when he said to her, "Beauty, will you be my wife?" For a few minutes she was not able to speak a word, for she was afraid of putting him in a passion by refusing. At length she said, "No, beast." The beast made no reply, but sighed deeply and went away. When Beauty found herself alone she began to feel pity for the poor beast. "Dear!" said she, "what a sad thing it is that he should be so very frightful since he is so good-tempered!"

Beauty lived three months in this palace, very well pleased. The beast came to see her every night, and talked with her while she supped; and though what he said was not very clever, yet she saw in him every day some new mark of his goodness, so instead of dreading the time of his coming, she was always looking at her watch to see if it was almost nine o'clock, for that was the time when he never failed to visit her. There was but one thing that vexed her: which was that every

"SHE SAW AT HER FEET, INSTEAD OF THE POOR BEAST, A HANDSOME PRINCE"

night before the beast went away from her, he always made it a rule to ask her if she would be his wife, and seemed very much grieved at her saying no. At last, one night, she said to him, "You vex me greatly, beast, by forcing me to refuse you so often; I wish I could take such a liking to you as to agree to marry you, but I must tell you plainly that I do not think it will ever happen. I shall always be your friend, so try to let that make you easy." "I must needs do so then," said the beast, "for I know well enough how frightful I am, but I love you better than myself. Yet I think I am very lucky in your being pleased to stay with me; now promise me, Beauty, that you will never leave me." Beauty was quite struck when he said this, for that very day she had seen in her glass that her father had fallen sick of grief for her sake, and was very ill for the want of seeing her again. "I would promise you with all my heart," said she, "never to leave you quite; but I long so much to see my father that if you do not give me leave to visit him I shall die with grief." "I would rather die myself, Beauty," answered the beast, "than make you fret; I will send you to your father's cottage, you shall stay there, and your poor beast shall die of sorrow."

"No," said Beauty, crying, "I love you too well to be the cause of your death; I promise to return in a week. You have shown me that my sisters are married, and my brothers are gone for soldiers, so that my father is left all alone. Let me stay a week with him." "You shall find yourself with him to-morrow morning," replied the beast; "but mind, do not forget your promise. When you wish to return you have nothing to do but to put your ring on a table when you go to bed. Good-bye, Beauty!" The beast then sighed as he said these words, and Beauty went to bed very sorry to see him so much grieved. When she awoke in the morning, she found herself in her father's cottage. She rung a bell that was at her bedside, and a servant entered; but as soon as she saw Beauty the woman gave a loud shriek; upon which the merchant ran upstairs, and when he beheld his daughter he was ready to die of joy. He ran to the bedside, and kissed her a hundred times. At last Beauty began to remember that she had brought no clothes with her to put on; but the servant told her she had just found in the next room a large chest full of dresses, trimmed all over with gold, and adorned with pearls and diamonds. Beauty in her own mind thanked the beast for his kindness, and put on the plainest gown she could find among them all. She then told the servant to put the rest away with a great deal of care, for she intended to give them to her sisters; but as soon as she had spoken these words the chest was gone out of sight in a moment. Her father then said, perhaps the beast chose for her to keep them all for herself; and as soon as he had said this, they saw the chest standing again in the same place. While Beauty was dressing herself a servant brought word to her that her sisters were come with their husbands to pay her a visit. They both lived unhappily with the gentlemen they had married. The husband of the eldest was very handsome; but was so very proud of this that he thought of nothing else from morning till night, and did not attend to the beauty of his wife. The second had married a man of great learning, but he made no use of it, only to torment and affront all his friends, and his wife more than any of them. The two sisters were ready to burst with spite when they saw Beauty dressed like a princess and look so very charming. All the kindness that she showed them was of no use, for they were vexed more than ever when she told them how happy she lived at the palace of the beast. The spiteful creatures went by themselves into the garden, where they cried to think of her good fortune. "Why should the little wretch be better off than we?" said they. "We are much handsomer than she is." "Sister," said the eldest, "a thought has just come into my head: let us try to keep her here longer than the week that the beast gave her leave for, and then he will be so angry that perhaps he will eat her up in a moment." "That is well thought of," answered the other, "but to do this we must seem very kind to her." They then made up their minds to be so, and went to join her in the cottage, where they showed her so much false love that Beauty could not help crying for joy.

When the week was ended, the two sisters began to pretend so much grief at the thoughts of her leaving them, that she agreed to stay a week more; but all that time Beauty could not help fretting for the sorrow that she knew her staying would give her poor beast, for she tenderly loved him, and much wished for his company again. The tenth night of her being at the cottage she dreamed she was in the garden of the palace, and that the beast lay dying on a grass plot, and, with his last breath, put her in mind of her promise and laid his death to her keeping away from him. Beauty awoke in a great fright and burst into tears. "Am not I wicked," said she, "to behave so ill to a beast who has shown me so much kindness; why will I not marry him? I am sure I should be more happy with him than my sisters are with their husbands. He shall not be wretched any longer on my account, for I should do nothing but blame myself all the rest of my life."

She then rose, put her ring on the table, got into bed again, and soon fell asleep. In the morning she with joy found herself in the palace of the beast. She dressed herself very finely that she might please him the better, and thought she had never known a day pass away so slow. At last the clock struck nine, but the beast did not come. Beauty then thought to be sure she had been the cause of his death in earnest. She ran from room to room all over the palace, calling out his name, but still she saw nothing of him. After looking for him a long time, she thought of her dream, and ran directly toward the grass plot; and there she found the poor beast lying senseless and seeming dead. She threw herself upon his body, thinking nothing at all of his ugliness, and finding his heart still beat, she ran and fetched some water from a pond in the garden and threw it on his face. The beast then opened his eyes, and said: "You have forgot your promise, Beauty. My grief for the loss of you has made me resolve to starve myself to death; but I shall die content, since I have had the pleasure of seeing you once more." "No, dear beast," replied Beauty, "you shall not die; you shall live to be my husband; from this moment I offer to marry you, and will be only yours. Oh! I thought I felt only friendship for you, but the pain I now feel shows me that I could not live without seeing you."

The moment Beauty had spoken these words the palace was suddenly lighted up, and music, fireworks, and all kinds of rejoicings appeared round about them. Yet Beauty took no notice of all this, but watched over her dear beast with the greatest tenderness. But now she was all at once amazed to see at her feet, instead of her poor beast, the handsomest prince that ever was seen, who thanked her most warmly for having broken his enchantment. Though this young prince deserved all her notice, she could not help asking him what was become of the beast. "You see him at your feet, Beauty," answered the prince, "for I am he. A wicked fairy had condemned me to keep the form of a beast till a beautiful young lady should agree to marry me, and ordered me, on pain of death, not to show that I had any sense. You, alone, dearest Beauty, have kindly judged of me by the goodness of my heart, and in return I offer you my hand and my crown, though I know the reward is much less than what I owe you." Beauty, in the most pleasing surprise, helped the prince to rise, and they walked along to the palace, when her wonder was very great to find her father and sisters there, who had been brought by the lady Beauty had seen in her dream. "Beauty," said the lady (for she was a fairy), "receive the reward of the choice you have made. You have chosen goodness of heart rather than sense and beauty; therefore you deserve to find them all three joined in the same person. You are going to be a great Queen; I hope a crown will not destroy your virtue."

As for you, ladies," said the fairy to the other two sisters, "I have long known the malice of your hearts, and the wrongs you have done. You shall become two statues, but under that form you shall still keep your reason, and shall be fixed at the gates of your sister's palace, and I will not pass any worse sentence on you than to see her happy. You will never appear in your own persons again till you are fully cured of your faults, and to tell the truth, I am very much afraid you will remain statues forever."

At the same moment, the fairy, with a stroke of her wand, removed all who were present to the young prince's country, where he was received with the greatest joy by his subjects. He married Beauty, and passed a long and happy life with her, because they still kept in the same course of goodness from which they had never departed.

Hansel and Grethel

NEAR the borders of a large forest dwelt in olden times a poor woodcutter, who had two children —a boy named Hansel, and his sister, Grethel. They had very little to live upon, and once, when there was a dreadful season of scarcity in the land, the poor woodcutter could not earn sufficient to supply their daily food.

One evening, after the children were gone to bed, the parents sat talking together over their sorrow, and the poor husband sighed and said to his wife, who was not the mother of his children, but their stepmother: "What will become of us, for I cannot earn enough to support myself and you, much less the children? what shall we do with them, for they must not starve."

HANSEL AND GRETHEL

"I know what to do, husband," she replied; "early to-morrow morning we will take the children for a walk across the forest and leave them in the thickest part; they will never find the way home again, you may depend, and then we shall only have to work for ourselves."

"No, wife," said the man, "that I will never do. How could I have the heart to leave my children all alone in the wood, where the wild beasts would come quickly and devour them?"

"Oh, you fool," replied the stepmother, "if you refuse to do this, you know we must all four perish with hunger; you may as well go and cut the wood for our coffins." And after this she let him have no peace till he became quite worn out, and could not sleep for hours, but lay thinking in sorrow about his children.

The two children, who also were too hungry to sleep, heard all that their stepmother had said to their father. Poor little Grethel wept bitter tears as she listened, and said to her brother, "What is going to happen to us, Hansel?"

"Hush, Grethel," he whispered; "don't be so unhappy. I know what to do."

Then they lay quite still till their parents were asleep. As soon as it was quiet, Hansel got up, put on his little coat, unfastened the door, and slipped out. The moon shone brightly, and the white pebble stones which lay

155

before the cottage door glistened like new silver money. Hansel stooped and picked up as many of the pebbles as he could stuff in his little coat pockets. He then went back to Grethel and said, "Be comforted, dear little sister, and sleep in peace; heaven will take care of us." Then he laid himself down again in bed, and slept till the day broke.

As soon as the sun was risen, the stepmother came and woke the two children, and said, "Get up, you lazy bones, and come into the wood with me to gather wood for the fire." Then she gave each of them a piece of bread, and said, "You must keep that to eat for your dinner, and don't quarrel over it for you will get nothing more."

Grethel took the bread under her charge, for Hansel's pockets were full of pebbles. Then the stepmother led them a long way into the forest. They had gone but a very short distance when Hansel looked back at the house, and this he did again and again.

At last his stepmother said, "Why do you keep staying behind and looking back so?"

"Oh, mother," said the boy, "I can see my little white cat sitting on the roof of the house, and I am sure she is crying for me."

"Nonsense," she replied; "that is not your cat; it is the morning sun shining on the chimney-pot."

Hansel had seen no cat, but he stayed behind every

time to drop a white pebble from his pocket on the ground as they walked.

As soon as they reached a thick part of the wood, their stepmother said:

"Come, children, gather some wood, and I will make a fire, for it is very cold here."

Then Hansel and Grethel raised quite a high heap of brushwood and faggots, which soon blazed up into a bright fire, and the woman said to them:

"Sit down here, children, and rest while I go and find your father, who is cutting wood in the forest; when we have finished our work, we will come again and fetch you."

Hansel and Grethel seated themselves by the fire, and when noon arrived they each ate the piece of bread which their stepmother had given them for their dinner; and as long as they heard the strokes of the axe they felt safe, for they believed that their father was working near them. But it was not an axe they heard—only a branch which still hung on a withered tree, and was moved up and down by the wind. At last, when they had been sitting there a long time, the children's eyes became heavy with fatigue, and they fell fast asleep. When they awoke it was dark night, and poor Grethel began to cry, and said, "Oh, how shall we get out of the wood?"

But Hansel comforted her. "Don't fear," he said, "let us wait a little while till the moon rises, and then we shall easily find our way home."

Very soon the full moon rose, and then Hansel took his little sister by the hand, and the white pebble stones, which glittered like newly coined money in the moonlight and which Hansel had dropped as he walked, pointed out the way. They walked all the night through, and did not reach their father's house till break of day.

They knocked at the door, and when their stepmother opened it, she exclaimed: "You naughty children, why have you been staying so long in the forest? We thought you were never coming back." But their father was overjoyed to see them, for it grieved him to the heart to think that they had been left alone in the wood.

Not long after this there came another time of scarcity and want in every house, and the children heard their stepmother talking after they were in bed. "The times are as bad as ever," she said; "we have just half a loaf left, and when that is gone all love will be at an end. The children must go away; we will take them deeper into the forest this time, and they will not be able to find their way home as they did before; it is the only plan to save ourselves from starvation." But the husband felt heavy at heart, for he thought it was better to share the last morsel with his children.

His wife would listen to nothing he said, but continued to reproach him, and as he had given way to her the first time, he could not refuse to do so now. The children were awake, and heard all the conversation; so, as soon as their parents slept, Hansel got up, intending to go out and gather some more of the bright pebbles to let fall as he walked, that they might point out the way home; but his stepmother had locked the door, and he could not open it. When he went back to his bed he told his little sister not to fret, but to go to sleep in peace, for he was sure they would be taken care of.

Early the next morning the stepmother came and pulled the children out of bed, and when they were dressed, gave them each a piece of bread for their dinners, smaller than they had had before, and then they started on their way to the wood.

As they walked, Hansel, who had the bread in his pocket, broke off little crumbs, and stopped every now and then to drop one, turning round as if he was looking back at his home.

"Hansel," said the woman, "what are you stopping for in that way?   Come along directly."

"I saw my pigeon sitting on the roof, and he wants to say good-bye to me," replied the boy.

"Nonsense," she said, "that is not your pigeon, it is only the morning sun shining on the chimney-top."

But Hansel did not look back any more; he only dropped pieces of bread behind him as they walked through the wood. This time they went on till they reached the thickest and densest part of the forest, where they had never been before in all their lives.

Again they gathered faggots and brushwood of which the stepmother made up a large fire. Then she said: "Remain here, children, and rest while I go to help your father, who is cutting wood in the forest; when you feel tired, you can lie down and sleep for a little while, and we will come and fetch you in the evening, when your father has finished his work."

So the children remained alone till midday, and then Grethel shared her piece of bread with Hansel, for he had scattered his own all along the road as they walked. After this they slept for a while, and the evening drew on; but no one came to fetch the poor children. When they awoke it was quite dark, and poor little Grethel was afraid; but Hansel comforted her, as he had done before, by telling her they need only wait till the moon rose. "You know, little sister," he said, "that I have thrown bread crumbs all along the road we came, and they will easily point out the way home."

But when they went out of the thicket into the moonlight they found no bread crumbs, for the numerous birds which inhabited the trees of the forest had picked them all up.

Hansel tried to hide his fear when he made this sad discovery, and said to his sister: "Cheer up, Grethel; I dare say we shall find our way home without the crumbs. Let us try." But this they found impossible. They wandered about the whole night, and the next day from

160

morning till evening; but they could not get out of the wood, and were so hungry that had it not been for a few berries which they picked they must have starved.

At last they were so tired that their poor little legs could carry them no farther; so they laid themselves down under a tree and went to sleep. When they awoke it was the third morning since they had left their father's house, and they determined to try once more to find their way home; but it was no use, they only went still deeper into the wood, and knew that if no help came they must starve.

About noon they saw a beautiful snow-white bird sitting on the branch of a tree, singing so beautifully that they stood still to listen. When he had finished his song, he spread out his wings and flew on before them. The children followed him, till at last they saw at a distance a small house, and the bird flew and perched on the roof.

But how surprised were the boy and girl, when they came nearer, to find that the house was built of gingerbread and ornamented with sweet cakes and tarts, while the window was formed of barley sugar. "Oh!" exclaimed Hansel, "let us stop here and have a splendid feast. I will have a piece from the roof first, Grethel; and you can eat some of the barley-sugar window, it tastes so nice." Hansel reached up on tiptoe, and breaking off a piece of the gingerbread he began to eat with all his might, for he was very hungry. Grethel seated herself on the doorstep, and began munching away at the cakes of which it was made. Presently a voice came out of the cottage:

> "Munching, crunching, munching,
> Who's eating up my house?"

Then answered the children:

> "The wind, the wind,
> Only the wind,"

and went on eating as if they never meant to leave off, without a suspicion of wrong. Hansel, who found the cake on the roof tasted very good, broke off another large piece, and Grethel had just taken out a whole pane of barley sugar from the window and seated herself to eat it, when the door opened, and a strange-looking old woman came out leaning on a stick.

Hansel and Grethel were so frightened that they let fall what they held in their hands. The old woman shook her head at them, and said: "Ah, you dear children, who has brought you here? Come in and stay with me for a little while, and there shall no harm happen to you." She seized them both by the hands as she spoke, and led them into the house. She gave them for supper plenty to eat and drink—milk and pancakes and sugar, apples and nuts; and when evening came, Hansel and Grethel were shown two beautiful little beds with white curtains, and they lay down in them and thought they were in heaven.

But although the old woman pretended to be friendly, she was a wicked witch, who had her house built of gingerbread on purpose to entrap children. When once they were in her power, she would feed them well till they got fat, and then kill them and cook them for her dinner; and this she called her feast-day. Fortunately the witch had weak eyes, and could not see very well; but she had a very keen scent, as wild animals have, and could easily discover when human beings were near. As Hansel and Grethel had approached her cottage, she laughed to herself maliciously, and said with a sneer: "I have them now; they shall not escape from me again!"

Early in the morning, before the children were awake, she was up, standing by their beds; and when she saw how beautiful they looked in their sleep, with their round rosy cheeks, she muttered to herself: "What nice tit-bits they will be!" Then she laid hold of Hansel with her rough hand, dragged him out of bed, and led him to a little cage which had a lattice door, and shut him in; he might scream as much as he would, but it was all useless.

After this she went back to Grethel, and shaking her roughly till she woke, cried: "Get up, you lazy hussy, and draw some water, that I may boil something good for your brother, who is shut up in a cage outside till he gets fat; and then I shall cook him and eat him!" When Grethel heard this she began to cry bitterly; but it was all useless, she was obliged to do as the wicked witch told her.

For poor Hansel's breakfast the best of everything was cooked; but Grethel had nothing for herself but a crab's claw. Every morning the old woman would go out to the little cage and say: "Hansel stick out your finger, that I may feel if you are fat enough for eating." But Hansel, who knew how dim her old eyes were, always stuck a bone through the bars of his cage, which she thought was his finger, for she could not see; and when she felt how thin it was, she wondered very much why he did not get fat.

However, as the weeks went on, and Hansel seemed not to get any fatter, she became impatient and said she could not wait any longer. "Go, Grethel," she cried to the maiden, "be quick and draw water; Hansel may be fat or lean, I don't care; to-morrow morning I mean to kill him and cook him!"

Oh! how the poor little sister grieved when she was forced to draw the water; and as the tears rolled down her cheeks, she exclaimed: "It would have been better to be eaten by wild beasts, or to have been starved to death in the woods; then we should have died together!"

"Stop your crying!" cried the old woman; "it is not of the least use; no one will come to help you."

Early in the morning Grethel was obliged to go out and fill the great pot with water, and hang it over the fire to boil. As soon as this was done, the old woman said: "We will bake some bread first; I have made the oven hot and the dough is already kneaded." Then she dragged poor Grethel up to the oven door, under which the flames were burning fiercely, and said: "Creep in there, and see if it is hot enough yet to bake the bread." But if Grethel had obeyed her, she would have shut the poor child in and baked her for dinner, instead of boiling Hansel.

Grethel, however, guessed what she wanted to do, and said: "I don't know how to get in through that narrow door."

"Stupid goose," said the old woman, "why, the oven door is quite large enough for me; just look, I could get in myself." As she spoke she stepped forward and pretended to put her head in the oven.

A sudden thought gave Grethel unusual strength; she started forward, gave the old woman a push which sent her right into the oven; then she shut the iron door and fastened the bolt.

Oh! how the old witch did howl; it was quite horrible to hear her. But Grethel ran away, and therefore she was left to burn, just as she had left many poor little children to burn. And how quickly Grethel ran to Hansel, opened the door of his cage, and cried: "Hansel, Hansel, we are free; the old witch is dead." He flew like a bird out of his cage at these words as soon as the door was opened, and the children were so overjoyed that they ran into each other's arms, and kissed each other with the greatest love.

And now that there was nothing to be afraid of, they went back into the house, and while looking round the old witch's room, they saw an old oak chest, which they opened and found it full of pearls and precious stones. "These are better than pebbles," said Hansel; and he filled his pockets as full as they would hold.

"I will carry some home too," said Grethel, and she held out her apron, which held quite as much as Hansel's pockets.

"We will go now," he said, "and get away as soon as we can from this enchanted forest."

They had been walking for nearly two hours when they came to a large sheet of water.

"What shall we do now?" said the boy. "We cannot get across, and there is no bridge of any sort."

"Oh! here comes a boat," cried Grethel, but she was mistaken; it was only a white duck which came swimming toward the children. "Perhaps she will help us across if we ask her," said the child; and she sang, "Little duck, do help poor Hansel and Grethel; there is not a bridge nor a boat—will you let us sail across on your white back?"

The good-natured duck came near the bank as Grethel spoke, so close indeed that Hansel could seat himself and wanted to take his little sister on his lap, but she said: "No, we shall be too heavy for the kind duck; let her take us over one at a time."

The good creature did as the children wished; she carried Grethel over first, and then came back for Hansel. And then how happy the children were to find themselves in a part of the wood which they remembered quite well, and as they walked on the more familiar it became, till at last they caught sight of their father's house. Then they began to run, and bursting into the room, threw themselves into their father's arms.

Poor man, he had not had a moment's peace since the children had been left alone in the forest; he was full of joy at finding them safe and well again, and now they had nothing to fear, for their wicked stepmother was dead.

But how surprised the poor woodcutter was, when Grethel opened and shook her little apron, to see the glittering pearls and precious stones scattered about the room, while Hansel drew handful after handful from his pockets. From this moment all his care and sorrow was at an end, and the father lived in happiness with his children till his death.

JACK THE GIANT KILLER

IN THE reign of the famous King Arthur, there
lived near the Land's End of England, in the
county of Cornwall, a worthy farmer who had
an only son named Jack. Jack was a boy of a bold
temper; he took pleasure in hearing or reading stories of
wizards, conjurers, giants, and fairies, and used to listen
eagerly while his father talked of the great deeds of the
brave knights of King Arthur's Round Table. When
Jack was sent to take care of the sheep and oxen in the
fields, he used to amuse himself with planning battles,
sieges, and the means to conquer or surprise a foe. He
was above the common sports of children; but hardly
any one could equal him at wrestling; or, if he met with

a match for himself in strength, his skill and address always made him the victor. In those days there lived on St. Michael's Mount of Cornwall, which rises out of the sea at some distance from the mainland, a huge giant. He was eighteen feet high and three yards round, and his fierce and savage looks were the terror of all his neighbours. He dwelt in a gloomy cavern on the very top of the mountain, and used to wade over to the mainland in search of his prey. When he came near, the people left their houses; and after he had glutted his appetite upon their cattle, he would throw half a dozen oxen upon his back, and tie three times as many sheep and hogs round his waist, and so march back to his own abode. The giant had done this for many years, and the coast of Cornwall was greatly hurt by his thefts, when Jack boldly resolved to destroy him. He therefore took a horn, a shovel, pickaxe, and a dark lantern, and early in a long winter's evening he swam to the mount. There he fell to work at once, and before morning he had dug a pit twenty-two feet deep and almost as many broad. He covered it over with sticks and straw, and strewed some of the earth over them to make it look just like solid ground. He then put his horn to his mouth, and blew such a loud and long tantivy, that the giant awoke and came toward Jack, roaring like thunder: "You saucy villain, you shall pay dearly for breaking my rest; I will broil you for my breakfast." He had scarcely spoken these words, when he came advancing one step farther; but then he tumbled headlong into the pit, and his fall shook the very mountain. "O ho, Mr. Giant!" said Jack, looking into the pit, "have you found your way so soon to the bottom? How is your appetite now? Will nothing serve you for breakfast this cold morning but broiling poor Jack?" The giant now tried to rise, but Jack struck him a blow on the crown of the head with his pickaxe, which killed him at once. Jack then made haste back to rejoice his friends with the news of the giant's death. When the justices of Cornwall heard of this valiant action, they sent for Jack, and declared that he should always be called Jack the Giant Killer; and they also gave him a sword and belt, upon which was written in letters of gold:

"This is the valiant Cornishman
Who slew the Giant Cormoran."

The news of Jack's exploits soon spread over the western parts of England; and another giant, called Old Blunderbore, vowed to have revenge on Jack, if it should ever be his fortune to get him into his power. This giant kept an enchanted castle in the midst of a lonely wood. About four months after the death of Cormoran, as Jack was taking a journey into Wales, he passed through this wood; and as he was very weary, he sat down to rest by the side of a pleasant fountain, and there he fell into a deep sleep. The giant came to the fountain for water just at this time, and found Jack there; and as the lines on Jack's belt showed who he was, the giant lifted him up and laid him gently upon his shoulder to carry him to his castle; but as he passed through the thicket, the rustling of the leaves waked Jack, and he was sadly afraid when he found himself in the clutches of Blunderbore. Yet this was nothing to his fright soon after; for when they reached the castle, he beheld the floor covered all over with the skulls and bones of men and women. The giant took him into a large room where lay the hearts and limbs of persons who had been lately killed; and he told Jack, with a horrid grin, that men's hearts, eaten with pepper and vinegar, were his nicest food; and also that he thought he should make a dainty meal on his heart. When he had said this, he locked Jack up in that room while he went to fetch another giant who lived in the same wood, to enjoy a dinner off Jack's flesh with him. While he was away, Jack heard dreadful shrieks, groans, and cries from many parts of the castle; and soon after he heard a mournful voice repeat these lines:

"Haste, valiant stranger, haste away,
　Lest you become the giant's prey.
　On his return he'll bring another,
　Still more savage than his brother:

A horrid, cruel monster, who,
Before he kills, will torture you.
Oh valiant stranger, haste away,
Or you'll become these giants' prey."

This warning was so shocking to poor Jack that he was ready to go mad. He ran to the window and saw the two giants coming along arm in arm. This window was right over the gates of the castle. "Now," thought Jack, "either my death or freedom is at hand." There were two strong cords in the room: Jack made a large noose with a slip-knot at the ends of both these, and as the giants were coming through the gates, he threw the ropes over their heads. He then made the other ends fast to a beam in the ceiling, and pulled with all his might till he had almost strangled them. When he saw that they were both quite black in the face and had not the least strength left, he drew his sword and slid down the ropes; he then killed the giants, and thus saved himself from the cruel death they meant to put him to. Jack next took a great bunch of keys from the pocket of Blunderbore, and went into the castle again. He made a strict search through all the rooms, and in them found three ladies tied up by the hair of their heads and almost starved to death. They told him that their husbands had been killed by the giants, who had then condemned them to be starved to death because they

172

would not eat the flesh of their own dead husbands. "Ladies," said Jack, "I have put an end to the monster and his wicked brother; and I give you this castle and all the riches it contains, to make you some amends for the dreadful pains you have felt." He then very politely gave them the keys of the castle, and went farther on his journey to Wales. As Jack had not taken any of the giant's riches for himself, and so had very little money of his own, he thought it best to travel as fast as he could. At length he lost his way, and when night came on he was in a lonely valley between two lofty mountains, where he walked about for some hours without seeing any dwelling-place, so he thought himself very lucky at last in finding a large and handsome house.

He went up to it boldly, and knocked loudly at the gate, when, to his great terror and surprise, there came forth a monstrous giant with two heads. He spoke to Jack very civilly, for he was a Welsh giant, and all the mischief he did was by private and secret malice under the show of friendship and kindness. Jack told him that he was a traveller who had lost his way, on which the huge monster made him welcome, and led him into a room where there was a good bed to pass the night in. Jack took off his clothes quickly; but though he was so weary he could not go to sleep. Soon after this he heard the giant walking backward and forward in the next room, and saying to himself:

"Though here you lodge with me this night,
You shall not see the morning light;
My club shall dash your brains out quite."

"Say you so?" thought Jack; "are these your tricks upon travellers? But I hope to prove as cunning as you." Then, getting out of bed, he groped about the room, and at last found a large thick billet of wood; he laid it in his own place in the bed, and then hid himself in a dark corner of the room. In the middle of the night the giant came with his great club, and struck many heavy blows on the bed, in the very place where Jack had laid the billet, and then he went back to his own room, thinking he had broken all his bones. Early in the morning, Jack put a bold face upon the matter, and walked into the giant's room to thank him for his lodgings. The giant started when he saw him and he began to stammer out: "Oh, dear me! Is it you? Pray how did you sleep last night? Did you hear or see anything in the dead of the night?" "Nothing worth speaking of," said Jack carelessly; "a rat, I believe, gave me three or four slaps with his tail, and disturbed me a little, but I soon went to sleep again." The giant wondered more and more at this; yet he did not answer a word, but went to bring two great bowls of hasty-pudding for their breakfast. Jack wished to make the giant believe that he could eat as much as himself, so he contrived to button a leathern bag inside his coat, and slipped the hasty-pudding into this bag while he seemed to put it into his mouth. When breakfast was over, he said to the giant: "Now I will show you a fine trick; I can cure all wounds with a touch; I could cut off my head one minute, and the next, put it sound again on my shoulders; you shall see an example." He then took hold of the knife, ripped up the leathern bag, and all the hasty-pudding tumbled out upon the floor. "Od splutter hur nails," cried the Welsh giant, who was ashamed to be outdone by such a little fellow as Jack, "hur can do that hurself.' So he snatched up the knife, plunged it into his stomach, and in a moment dropped down dead.

As soon as Jack had thus tricked the Welsh monster, he went farther on his journey; and a few days after he met with King Arthur's only son, who had got his father's leave to travel into Wales, to deliver a beautiful lady from the power of a wicked magician, who held her in his enchantments. When Jack found that the young prince had no servants with him, he begged leave to attend him; and the prince at once agreed to this, and gave Jack many thanks for his kindness. The prince was a handsome, polite, and brave knight, and so good-natured that he gave money to everybody he met. At length he gave his last penny to an old woman, and then turned to Jack and said: "How shall we be able to get food for ourselves the rest of our journey?" "Leave that to me, sir," said Jack; "I will provide for my prince." Night now came on, and the prince began to grow uneasy at thinking where they should lodge. "Sir," said Jack, "be of good heart; two miles farther there lives a large giant, whom I know well. He has three heads, and will fight five hundred men and make them fly before him." "Alas!" replied the king's son, "we had better never have been born than meet with such a monster." "My lord, leave me to manage him, and wait here in quiet till I return." The prince now stayed behind, while Jack rode on at full speed, and when he came to the gates of the castle, he gave a loud knock. The giant, with a voice like thunder, roared out: "Who is there?" And Jack made answer, and said: "No one but your poor cousin Jack." "Well," said the giant, "what news, cousin Jack?" "Dear uncle," said Jack, "I have some heavy news." "Pooh!" said the giant, "what heavy news can come to me? I am a giant with three heads, and can fight five hundred men, and make them fly before me." "Alas!" said Jack, "here is the king's son coming with two thousand men, to kill you and to destroy the castle and all that you have." "Oh, Cousin Jack," said the giant, "this is heavy news indeed! But I have a large cellar under ground, where I will hide myself, and you shall lock and bar me in, and keep the keys till the king's son is gone."

JACK THE GIANT KILLER

Now when Jack had made the giant fast in the vault, he went back and fetched the prince to the castle; they both made themselves merry with the wine and other dainties that were in the house. So that night they rested very pleasantly, while the poor giant lay trembling and shaking with fear in the cellar under ground. Early in the morning Jack gave the king's son gold and silver out of the giant's treasure, and set him three miles forward on his journey. He then went to let his uncle out of the hole, who asked Jack what he should give him as a reward for saving his castle. "Why, good uncle," said Jack, "I desire nothing but the old coat and cap, with the old rusty sword and slippers, which are hanging at your bed's head." Then said the giant: "You shall have them; and pray keep them for my sake, for they are things of great use: the coat will keep you invisible, the cap will give you knowledge, the sword cut through anything, and the shoes are of vast swiftness; these may be useful to you in all times of danger, so take them with all my heart." Jack gave many thanks to the giant, and then set off to the prince. When he had come up with the king's son, they soon arrived at the dwelling of the beautiful lady who was under the power of a wicked magician. She received the prince very politely, and made a noble feast for him; and when it was ended, she rose, and wiping her mouth with a fine handkerchief, said: "My lord, you must submit to the custom of my palace; to-morrow morning I command you to tell me on whom I bestow this handkerchief or lose your head." She then went out of the room. The young prince went to bed very mournful, but Jack put on his cap of knowledge, which told him that the lady was forced, by the power of enchantment, to meet the wicked magician every night in the middle of the forest. Jack now put on his coat of darkness and his shoes of swiftness, and was there before her. When the lady came, she gave the handkerchief to the magician. Jack, with his sword of sharpness, at one blow cut off his head; the enchantment was then ended in a moment, and the lady was restored to her former virtue and goodness.

She was married to the prince on the next day, and soon after went back with her royal husband and a great company to the court of King Arthur, where they were received with loud and joyful welcomes; and the valiant hero Jack, for the many great exploits he had done for the good of his country, was made one of the Knights of the Round Table. As Jack had been so unlucky in all his adventures, he resolved not to be idle for the future, but still to do what services he could for the honour of the king and the nation. He therefore humbly begged his Majesty to furnish him with a horse and money, that he might travel in search of new and strange exploits. "For," said he to the king, "there are many giants yet

JACK THE GIANT KILLER

living in the remote parts of Wales, to the great terror and
distress to your Majesty's subjects; therefore, if it please
you, sire, to favour me in my design, I will soon rid your
kingdom of these giants and monsters in human shape."
Now when the king heard this offer and began to think
of the cruel deeds of these bloodthirsty giants and
savage monsters, he gave Jack everything proper for
such a journey. After this Jack took leave of the king,
the prince, and all the knights, and set off, taking with
him his cap of knowledge, his sword of sharpness, his
shoes of swiftness, and his invisible coat, the better to
perform the great exploits that might fall in his way.
He went along over high hills and lofty mountains, and
on the third day he came to a large wide forest, through
which his road led. He had hardly entered the forest,
when, on a sudden, he heard very dreadful shrieks and
cries. He forced his way through the trees, and saw a
monstrous giant dragging along by the hair of their
heads a handsome knight and his beautiful lady. Their
tears and cries melted the heart of honest Jack to pity
and compassion; he alighted from his horse, and, tying
him to an oak tree, he put on his invisible coat, under
which he carried his sword of sharpness.

When he came up to the giant, he made several
strokes at him, but could not reach his body on account
of the enormous height of the terrible creature, but he
wounded his thighs in several places; and at length,

179

putting both hands to his sword, and aiming with all his might, he cut off both the giant's legs just below the garter, and the trunk of his body tumbling to the ground made not only the trees shake, but the earth itself tremble with the force of his fall. Then Jack, setting his foot upon his neck, exclaimed: "Thou barbarous and savage wretch, behold I come to execute upon thee the just reward for all thy crimes"; and instantly plunged his sword into the giant's body. The huge monster gave a hideous groan, and yielded up his life into the hands of the victorious Jack the Giant Killer, whilst the noble knight and the virtuous lady were both joyful spectators of his sudden death and their deliverance. The courteous knight and his fair lady, not only returned Jack hearty thanks for their deliverance, but also invited him to their house, to refresh himself after his dreadful encounter, as likewise to receive a reward for his good services. "No," said Jack, "I cannot be at ease till I find out the den that was the monster's habitation." The knight on hearing this grew very sorrowful, and replied: "Noble stranger, it is too much to run a second hazard; this monster lived in a den under yonder mountain, with a brother of his more fierce and cruel than himself; therefore, if you should go thither and perish in the attempt, it would be a heartbreaking thing to me and my lady; so let me persuade you to go with us, and desist from any further pursuit." "Nay," answered Jack, "if there be another, even if there were twenty, I would shed the last drop of blood in my body before one of them should escape my fury. When I have finished this task, I will come and pay my respects to you." So when they had told him where to find them again, he got on his horse and went after the dead giant's brother.

Jack had not ridden a mile and a half before he came in sight of the mouth of the cavern; and nigh the entrance of it he saw the other giant sitting on a huge block of fine timber, with a knotted iron club lying by his side, waiting for his brother. His eyes looked like flames of fire, his face was grim and ugly, and his cheeks seemed like two flitches of bacon; the bristles of his beard seemed to be thick rods of iron wire, and his long locks of hair hung down upon his broad shoulders like curling snakes. Jack got down from his horse and turned him into a thicket; then he put on his coat of darkness, and drew a little nearer to behold this figure, and said softly: "Oh, monster! are you there? It will not be long before I shall take you fast by the beard." The giant all this while could not see him by reason of his invisible coat, so Jack came quite close to him, and struck a blow at his head with his sword of sharpness, but he missed his aim and cut off only his nose, which made him roar like loud claps of thunder. And though he rolled his glaring eyes round on every side, he could not see who had given

181

him the blow; yet he took up his iron club, and began to lay about him like one that was mad with pain and fury.

"Nay," said Jack, "if this be the case I will kill you at once." So saying he slipped nimbly behind him, and jumping upon the block of timber, as the giant rose from it, he stabbed him in the back, when, after a few howls, he dropped down dead. Jack cut off his head, and sent it with the head of his brother, whom he had killed before in the forest, to King Arthur, by a wagon which he hired for that purpose, with an account of all his exploits. When Jack had thus killed these two monsters, he went into their cave in search of their treasure; he passed through many turnings and windings, which led him to a room paved with freestone; at the end of it was a boiling caldron, and on the right hand stood a large table where the giants used to dine. He then came to a window that was secured with iron bars, through which he saw a number of wretched captives, who cried out when they saw Jack: "Alas! alas! young man, you are come to be one among us in this horrid den." "I hope," said Jack, "you will not stay here long; but pray tell me what is the meaning of your being here at all?" "Alas!" said one poor old man, "I will tell you, sir. We are persons that have been taken by the giants who hold this cave, and are kept till they choose to have a feast; then one of us is to be killed, and cooked to please their taste. It is not long since they took three for the same purpose."

"Well," said Jack, "I have given them such a dinner
that it will be long enough before they have any more."
The captives were amazed at his words. "You may believe me," said Jack; "for I have killed them both with
the edge of the sword, and have sent their large heads to
the court of King Arthur as marks of my great success.

To show them that what he said was true, he unlocked
the gate and set them all free. Then he led them to the
great room, placed them round the table, and set before
them two quarters of beef, with bread and wine, upon
which they feasted to their fill. When supper was over,
they searched the giants' coffers, and Jack shared the
store in them among the captives, who thanked him for
their escape. The next morning they set off to their
homes, and Jack to the knight's house, whom he had left
with his lady not long before. It was just at the time of
sunrise that Jack mounted his horse to proceed on his
journey.

He arrived at the knight's house, where he was received with the greatest joy by the thankful knight and
his lady, who, in honour of Jack's exploits, gave a grand
feast, to which all the nobles and gentry were invited.
When the company were assembled, the knight declared
to them the great actions of Jack, and gave him, as a
mark of respect, a fine ring, on which was engraved the

picture of the giant dragging the knight and the lady by the hair, with this motto around it:

> "Behold, in dire distress were we,
>   Under a giant's fierce command;
>   But gained our lives and liberty,
>   From valiant Jack's victorious hand."

Among the guests then present were five aged gentlemen, who were fathers to some of those captives who had been freed by Jack from the dungeon of the giants. As soon as they heard that he was the person who had done such wonders, they pressed around him with tears of joy, to return him thanks for the happiness he had caused to them. After this the bowl went round, and every one drank to the health and long life of the gallant hero. Mirth increased, and the hall was filled with peals of laughter and joyful cries. But, on a sudden, a herald, pale and breathless with haste and terror, rushed into the midst of the company, and told them that Thundel, a savage giant with two heads, had heard of the death of his two kinsmen, and was come to take his revenge on Jack; and that he was now within a mile of the house, the people flying before him like chaff before the wind. At this news the very boldest of the guests trembled; but Jack drew his sword, and said: "Let him come, I have a rod for him also. Pray, ladies and gentlemen, do me the favour to walk into the garden, and you will soon behold the giant's defeat and death." To this they all agreed, and heartily wished him success in his dangerous attempt. The knight's house stood in the middle of a moat, thirty feet deep and twenty wide, over which lay a drawbridge. Jack set men to work to cut the bridge on both sides, almost to the middle, and then dressed himself in his coat of darkness, and went against the giant with his sword of sharpness. As he came close to him, though the giant could not see him for his invisible coat, yet he found some danger was near, which made him cry out:

"Fa, fe, fi, fo, fum,
 I smell the blood of an Englishman;
 Let him be alive, or let him be dead,
 I'll grind his bones to make me bread."

"Say you so my friend?" said Jack. "You are a monstrous miller indeed." "Art thou," cried the giant, "the villain that killed my kinsmen? Then I will tear thee with my teeth and grind thy bones to powder." "You must catch me first," said Jack; and throwing off his coat of darkness and putting on his shoes of swiftness, he began to run, the giant following him like a walking castle, making the earth shake at every step.

Jack led him round and round the walls of the house,

that the company might see the monster; and to finish
the work Jack ran over the drawbridge, the giant going
after him with his club. But when the giant came to
the middle, where the bridge had been cut on both sides,
the great weight of his body made it break, and he
tumbled into the water and rolled about like a large
whale. Jack now stood by the side of the moat, and
laughed and jeered at him, saying: "I think you told me
you would grind my bones to powder. When will you
begin?" The giant foamed at both his horrid mouths
with fury, and plunged from side to side of the moat;
but he could not get out to have revenge on his little
foe. At last Jack ordered a cart rope to be brought to
him. He then drew it over his two heads, and by the
help of a team of horses, dragged him to the edge of the
moat, where he cut off the monster's heads; and before
he either ate or drank, he sent them both to the court of
King Arthur. He then went back to the table with the
company, and the rest of the day was spent in mirth and
good cheer. After staying with the knight for some
time, Jack grew weary of such an idle life, and set out
again in search of new adventures. He went over the
hills and dales without meeting any till he came to the
foot of a very high mountain. Here he knocked at the
door of a small and lonely house, and an old man, with a
head as white as snow, let him in. "Good father," said
Jack, "can you lodge a traveller who has lost his way?"

"Yes," said the hermit, "I can if you will accept such fare as my poor house affords." Jack entered, and the old man set before him some bread and fruit for his supper. When Jack had eaten as much as he chose, the hermit said: "My son, I know you are the famous conqueror of giants; now on the top of this mountain is an enchanted castle, kept by a giant named Galligantus, who, by the help of a vile magician, gets many knights into his castle, where he changes them into the shape of beasts. Above all I lament the hard fate of a duke's daughter, whom they seized as she was walking in her father's garden, and brought hither through the air in a chariot drawn by two fiery dragons, and turned her into the shape of a deer. Many knights have tried to destroy the enchantment and deliver her; yet none have been able to do it, by reason of two fiery griffins who guard the gate of the castle and destroy all who come nigh. But as you, my son, have an invisible coat, you may pass by them without being seen; and on the gates of the castle you will find engraved by what means the enchantment may be broken."

Jack promised that in the morning, at the risk of his life, he would break the enchantment; and after a sound sleep he arose early, put on his invisible coat, and got ready for the attempt. When he had climbed to the top of the mountain, he saw the two fiery griffins; but he passed between them without the least fear of danger, for they could not see him because of his invisible coat. On the castle gate he found a golden trumpet, under which was written these lines:

"Whoever can this trumpet blow,
    Shall cause the giant's overthrow."

As soon as Jack had read this, he seized the trumpet, and blew a shrill blast which made the gates fly open and the very castle itself tremble. The giant and the conjurer now knew that their wicked course was at an end, and they stood biting their thumbs and shaking with fear. Jack, with his sword of sharpness, soon killed the giant. The magician was then carried away by a whirlwind, and every knight and beautiful lady who had been changed into birds and beasts, returned to their proper shapes. The castle vanished away like smoke, and the head of the giant Galligantus was sent to King Arthur. The knights and ladies rested that night at the old man's hermitage, and next day they set out for the court. Jack then went up to the king, and gave his Majesty an account of all his fierce battles. Jack's fame had spread through the whole country; and at the king's desire, the duke gave him his daughter in marriage, to the joy of all the kingdom. After this the king gave him a large estate; on which he and his lady lived the rest of their days in joy and content.

THE SECOND VOYAGE OF SINDBAD THE SAILOR

I DESIGNED, after my first voyage, to spend the rest of my days at Bagdad, but it was not long ere I grew weary of an indolent life, and I put to sea a second time, with merchants of known probity. We embarked on board a good ship and, after recommending ourselves to God, set sail. We traded from island to island, and exchanged commodities with great profit. One day we landed on an island covered with several sorts of fruit trees, but we could see neither man nor animal. We walked in the meadows, along the streams that watered them. While some diverted themselves with gathering flowers, and others fruit, I took my wine and provisions, and sat down near a stream betwixt two

189

high trees which formed a thick shade. I made a good meal, and afterward fell asleep. I cannot tell how long I slept but when I awoke the ship was gone.

In this sad condition I was ready to die with grief. I cried out in agony, beat my head and breast, and threw myself upon the ground, where I lay some time in despair. I upbraided myself a hundred times for not being content with the produce of my first voyage, that might have sufficed me all my life. But all this was in vain, and my repentance came too late. At last I resigned myself to the will of God. Not knowing what to do, I climbed up to the top of a lofty tree, from whence I looked about on all sides, to see if I could discover anything that could give me hopes. When I gazed toward the sea I could see nothing but sky and water; but looking over the land, I beheld something white; and coming down, I took what provision I had left and went toward it, the distance being so great that I could not distinguish what it was.

As I approached, I thought it to be a white dome of a prodigious height and extent; and when I came up to it, I touched it and found it to be very smooth. I went round to see if it was open on any side, but saw it was not, and that there was no climbing up to the top, as it was so smooth. It was at least fifty paces round.

By this time the sun was about to set, and all of a sudden the sky became as dark as if it had been covered with a thick cloud. I was much astonished at this sudden darkness, but much more when I found it occasioned by a bird of a monstrous size that came flying toward me. I remembered that I had often heard mariners speak of a miraculous bird called the roc, and conceived that the great dome which I so much admired must be its egg. In short, the bird alighted and sat over the egg. As I perceived her coming, I crept close to the egg, so that I had before me one of the legs of the bird, which was as big as the trunk of a tree. I tied myself strongly to it with my turban, in hopes that the roc next morning would carry me with her out of this desert island. After having passed the night in this condition, the bird flew away as soon as it was daylight, and carried me so high that I could not discern the earth; she afterward descended with so much rapidity that I lost my senses. But when I found myself on the ground I speedily untied the knot, and had scarcely done so, when the roc, having taken up a serpent of a monstrous length in her bill, flew away.

The spot where it left me was encompassed on all sides by mountains that seemed to reach above the clouds, and so steep that there was no possibility of getting out of the valley. This was a new perplexity; so that when I compared this place with the desert island from which the roc had brought me, I found that I had gained nothing by the change.

As I walked through this valley, I perceived it was strewed with diamonds, some of which were of surprising bigness. I took pleasure in looking upon them; but shortly saw at a distance such objects as greatly diminished my satisfaction, and which I could not view without terror; namely, a great number of serpents, so monstrous that the least of them was capable of swallowing an elephant. They retired in the daytime to their dens, where they hid themselves from the roc, their enemy, and came out only in the night.

I spent the day in walking about in the valley, resting myself at times in such places as I thought most convenient. When night came on I went into a cave, where I thought I might repose in safety. I secured the entrance, which was low and narrow, with a great stone to preserve me from the serpents, but not so far as to exclude the light. I supped on part of my provisions, but the serpents, which began hissing round me, put me into such extreme fear that I did not sleep. When day appeared the serpents retired; and I came out of the cave trembling. I can justly say that I walked upon diamonds without feeling any inclination to touch them. At last I sat down, and notwithstanding my apprehensions, not having closed my eyes during the night, fell asleep, after having eaten a little more of my provisions. But I had scarcely shut my eyes when something that fell by me with a great noise awakened me.

This was a large piece of raw meat, and at the same time I saw several others fall down from the rocks in different places.

I had always regarded as fabulous what I had heard sailors and others relate of the valley of diamonds, and of the stratagems employed by merchants to obtain jewels from thence; but now I found that they had stated nothing but the truth. For the fact is, that the merchants come to the neighbourhood of this valley, when the eagles have young ones, and throwing great joints of meat into the valley, the diamonds, upon whose points they fall, stick to them; the eagles, which are stronger in this country than anywhere else, pounce with great force upon those pieces of meat, and carry them to their nests on the precipices of the rocks to feed their young: the merchants at this time run to their nests, disturb and drive off the eagles by their shouts, and take away the diamonds that stick to the meat.

I perceived in this device the means of my deliverance.

Having collected together the largest diamonds I could find, I put them into the leather bag in which I used to carry my provisions. I took the largest of the pieces of meat, tied it close around me with the cloth of my turban, and then laid myself upon the ground, with my face downward, the bag of diamonds being made fast to my girdle.

I had scarcely placed myself in this posture when one

of the eagles, having taken me up with the piece of meat to which I was fastened, carried me to his nest on the top of the mountain. The merchants immediately began their shouting to frighten the eagles; and when they had obliged them to quit their prey, one of them came to the nest where I was. He was much alarmed when he saw me; but recovering himself, instead of inquiring how I came thither, began to quarrel with me, and asked why I stole his goods. "You will treat me," replied I, "with more civility when you know me better. Do not be uneasy; I have diamonds enough for you and myself, more than all the other merchants together. Whatever they have they owe to chance; but I selected for myself, in the bottom of the valley, those which you see in this bag." I had scarcely done speaking, when the other merchants came crowding about us, much astonished to see me; but they were much more surprised when I told them my story.

They conducted me to their encampment, and there, having opened my bag, they were surprised at the largeness of my diamonds, and confessed that they had never seen any of such size and perfection. I prayed the merchant who owned the nest to which I had been carried (for every merchant had his own), to take as many for his share as he pleased. He contented himself with one, and that, too, the least of them; and when I pressed him to take more without fear of doing me any injury: "No," said he, "I am very well satisfied with this, which is valuable enough to save me the trouble of making any more voyages, and will raise as great a fortune as I desire."

I spent the night with the merchants, to whom I related my story a second time, for the satisfaction of those who had not heard it. I could not moderate my joy when I found myself delivered from the danger I have mentioned. I thought myself in a dream, and could scarcely believe myself out of danger.

The merchants had thrown their pieces of meat into the valley for several days; and each of them being satisfied with the diamonds that had fallen to his lot, we left the place the next morning and travelled near high mountains, where there were serpents of a prodigious length, which we had the good fortune to escape. We took shipping at the first port we reached, and touched at the isle of Roha, where the trees grow that yield camphire. This tree is so large and its branches so thick, that one hundred men may easily sit under its shade. The juice, of which the camphire is made, exudes from a hole bored in the upper part of the tree, and is received in a vessel, where it thickens to a consistency, and becomes what we call camphire. After the juice is thus drawn out, the tree withers and dies.

In this island is also found the rhinoceros, an animal less than the elephant, but larger than the buffalo. It has a horn upon its nose, about a cubit in length; this horn is solid, and cleft through the middle. The rhinoceros fights with the elephant, runs his horn into his belly, and carries him off upon his head; but the blood and the fat of the elephant running into his eyes and making him blind, he falls to the ground; and then, strange to relate, the roc comes and carries them both away in her claws, for food for her young ones.

I pass over many other things peculiar to this island, lest I should weary you. Here I exchanged some of my diamonds for merchandise. From thence we went to other islands, and at last, having touched at several trading towns of the continent, we landed at Bussorah, from whence I proceeded to Bagdad. There I immediately gave large presents to the poor, and lived honourably upon the vast riches I had brought, and gained with so much fatigue.

Thus Sindbad ended the relation of the second voyage, gave Hindbad another hundred sequins, and invited him to come the next day to hear the account of the third.

The Story of Aladdin; or, the Wonderful Lamp

IN ONE of the large and rich cities of China there
once lived a tailor named Mustapha. He was very
poor. He could hardly, by his daily labour, maintain himself and his family, which consisted only of his
wife and a son.

His son, who was called Aladdin, was a very careless
and idle fellow. He was disobedient to his father and
mother, and would go out early in the morning and
stay out all day, playing in the streets and public places
with idle children of his own age.

When he was old enough to learn a trade, his father
took him into his own shop and taught him how to use
his needle; but all his father's endeavours to keep him to

his work were vain, for no sooner was his back turned, than he was gone for that day. Mustapha chastised him, but Aladdin was incorrigible, and his father, to his great grief, was forced to abandon him to his idleness; and was so much troubled about him, that he fell sick and died in a few months.

Aladdin, who was now no longer restrained by the fear of a father, gave himself entirely over to his idle habits, and was never out of the streets from his companions. This course he followed till he was fifteen years old, without giving his mind to any useful pursuit or the least reflection on what would become of him. As he was one day playing, according to custom, in the street with his evil associates, a stranger passing by stood to observe him.

This stranger was a sorcerer, known as the African magician, as he had been but two days arrived from Africa, his native country.

The African magician, observing in Aladdin's countenance something which assured him that he was a fit boy for his purpose, inquired his name and history of some of his companions, and when he had learnt all he desired to know, went up to him, and taking him aside from his comrades, said: "Child, was not your father called Mustapha, the tailor?" "Yes, sir," answered the boy, "but he has been dead a long time."

At these words the African magician threw his arms

about Aladdin's neck, and kissed him several times with tears in his eyes, and said: "I am your uncle. Your worthy father was my own brother. I knew you at first sight, you are so like him." Then he gave Aladdin a handful of small money, saying, "Go, my son, to your mother, give my love to her, and tell her that I will visit her to-morrow, that I may see where my good brother lived so long and ended his days."

Aladdin ran to his mother, overjoyed at the money his uncle had given him. "Mother," said he, "have I an uncle?" "No, child," replied his mother, "you have no uncle by your father's side or mine." "I am just now come," said Aladdin, "from a man who says he is my uncle and my father's brother. He cried and kissed me when I told him my father was dead, and gave me money, sending his love to you, and promising to come and pay you a visit, that he may see the house my father lived and died in." "Indeed, child," replied the mother, "your father had no brother, nor have you an uncle."

The next day the magician found Aladdin playing in another part of the town, and embracing him as before, put two pieces of gold into his hand, and said to him: "Carry this, child, to your mother; tell her that I will come and see her to-night, and bid her get us something for supper; but first show me the house where you live."

Aladdin showed the African magician the house, and carried the two pieces of gold to his mother, who went out and bought provisions; and, considering she wanted various utensils, borrowed them of her neighbours. She spent the whole day in preparing the supper; and at night, when it was ready, said to her son: "Perhaps the stranger knows not how to find our house; go and bring him, if you meet with him."

Aladdin was just ready to go, when the magician knocked at the door, and came in loaded with wine and all sorts of fruits, which he brought for a dessert. After he had given what he brought into Aladdin's hands, he saluted his mother, and desired her to show him the place where his brother Mustapha used to sit on the sofa; and when she had so done, he fell down and kissed it several times, crying out, with tears in his eyes: "My poor brother! how unhappy am I, not to have come soon enough to give you one last embrace." Aladdin's mother desired him to sit down in the same place, but he declined. "No," said he, "I shall not do that; but give me leave to sit opposite to it, that although I see not the master of a family so dear to me, I may at least behold the place where he used to sit."

When the magician had made choice of a place and sat down, he began to enter into discourse with Aladdin's mother. "My good sister," said he, "do not be surprised at your never having seen me all the time you have been married to my brother Mustapha of happy memory. I have been forty years absent from this country, which is my native place as well as my late brother's, and during that time have travelled into the Indies, Persia, Arabia, Syria, and Egypt, and afterward crossed over into Africa, where I took up my abode. At last, as it is natural for a man, I was desirous to see my native country again, and to embrace my dear brother; and finding I had strength enough to undertake so long a journey, I made the necessary preparations and set out. Nothing ever afflicted me so much as hearing of my brother's death. But God be praised for all things! It is a comfort for me to find, as it were, my brother in a son who has his most remarkable features."

The African magician perceiving that the widow wept at the remembrance of her husband, changed the conversation and, turning toward her son, asked him: "What business do you follow? Are you of any trade?"

At this question the youth hung down his head, and was not a little abashed when his mother answered: "Aladdin is an idle fellow. His father, when alive, strove all he could to teach him his trade, but could not succeed; and since his death, notwithstanding all I can say to him, he does nothing but idle away his time in the streets, as you saw him, without considering he is no longer a child; and if you do not make him ashamed of it, I despair of his ever coming to any good. For my part, I am resolved, one of these days, to turn him out of doors and let him provide for himself."

After these words, Aladdin's mother burst into tears; and the magician said: "This is not well, nephew; you must think of helping yourself and getting your livelihood. There are many sorts of trades; perhaps you do not like your father's, and would prefer another; I will endeavour to help you. If you have no mind to learn any handicraft, I will take a shop for you, furnish it with all sorts of fine stuffs and linens; and then with the money you make of them you can lay in fresh goods, and live in an honourable way. Tell me freely what you think of my proposal; you shall always find me ready to keep my word."

This plan just suited Aladdin, who hated work. He told the magician he had a greater inclination to that business than to any other, and that he should be much obliged to him for his kindness. "Well, then," said the African magician, "I will carry you with me to-morrow, clothe you as handsomely as the best merchants in the city, and afterward we will open a shop as I mentioned."

The widow, after his promises of kindness to her son, no longer doubted that the magician was her husband's brother. She thanked him for his good intentions, and after having exhorted Aladdin to render himself worthy of his uncle's favour, served up supper, at which they talked of several indifferent matters; and then the magician took his leave and retired.

He came again the next day, as he had promised, and took Aladdin with him to a merchant who sold all sorts of clothes for different ages and ranks, ready made, and a variety of fine stuffs, and bade Aladdin choose those he preferred, which he paid for.

When Aladdin found himself so handsomely equipped, he returned his uncle thanks, who thus addressed him: "As you are soon to be a merchant, it is proper you should frequent these shops, and be acquainted with them." He then showed him the largest and finest mosques, carried him to the khans or inns where the merchants and travellers lodged, and afterward to the sultan's palace, where he had free access; and at last brought him to his own khan, where, meeting with some merchants he had become acquainted with since his arrival, he gave them a treat, to bring them and his pretended nephew together.

This entertainment lasted till night, when Aladdin would have taken leave of his uncle to go home; the magician would not let him go by himself, but conducted him to his mother, who, as soon as she saw him so well dressed, was transported with joy, and bestowed a thousand blessings upon the magician.

Early the next morning the magician called again for Aladdin, and said he would take him to spend that day in the country, and on the next he would purchase the shop. He then led him out at one of the gates of the city, to some magnificent palaces, to each of which belonged beautiful gardens, into which anybody might enter. At every building he came to, he asked Aladdin if he did not think it fine; and the youth was ready to answer when any one presented itself, crying out: "Here is a finer house, uncle, than any we have yet seen." By this artifice the cunning magician led Aladdin some way into the country; and as he meant to carry him farther to execute his design, he took an opportunity to sit down in one of the gardens, on the brink of a fountain of clear water, which discharged itself by a lion's mouth of bronze into a basin, pretending to be tired. "Come, nephew," said he, "you must be weary as well as I. Let us rest ourselves, and we shall be better able to pursue our walk."

The magician next pulled from his girdle a handkerchief with cakes and fruit, and during this short repast he exhorted his nephew to leave off bad company and to seek that of wise and prudent men, to improve by their conversation; "for," said he, "you will soon be at man's estate, and you cannot too early begin to imitate their example." When they had eaten as much as they liked, they got up and pursued their walk through gardens separated from one another only by small ditches, which marked out the limits without interrupting the communication; so great was the confidence the inhabitants reposed in each other. By this means the African magician drew Aladdin insensibly beyond the gardens and crossed the country, till they nearly reached the mountains.

At last they arrived between two mountains of moderate height and equal size, divided by a narrow valley, which was the place where the magician intended to execute the design that had brought him from Africa to China. "We will go no farther now," said he to Aladdin; "I will show you here some extraordinary things, which, when you have seen, you will thank me for: but while I strike a light gather up all the loose dry sticks you can see, to kindle a fire with."

Aladdin found so many dried sticks, that he soon collected a great heap. The magician presently set them on fire, and when they were in a blaze, threw in some incense, pronouncing several magical words which Aladdin did not understand.

He had scarcely done so when the earth opened just before the magician, and discovered a stone with a brass ring fixed in it. Aladdin was so frightened that he would have run away, but the magician caught hold of him, and gave him such a box on the ear that he knocked him down. Aladdin got up trembling, and with tears in his eyes said to the magician, "What have I done, uncle, to be treated in this severe manner?" "I am your uncle," answered the magician: "I supply the place of your father, and you ought to make no reply. But child," added he, softening, "do not be afraid; for I shall not ask anything of you but that you obey me punctually, if you would reap the advantages which I intend you. Know, then, that under this stone there is hidden a treasure, destined to be yours, and which will make you richer than the greatest monarch in the world. No person but yourself is permitted to lift this stone or enter the cave; so you must punctually execute what I may command, for it is a matter of great consequence both to you and me."

Aladdin, amazed at all he saw and heard, forgot what was past, and rising said: "Well, uncle, what is to be done? Command me, I am ready to obey." "I am overjoyed, child," said the African magician, embracing him. "Take hold of the ring, and lift up that stone." "Indeed, uncle," replied Aladdin, "I am not strong enough; you must help me." "You have no occasion for my assistance," answered the magician. "If I help you, we shall be able to do nothing. Take hold of the ring, and lift it up; you will find it will come easily." Aladdin did as the magician bade him, raised the stone with ease, and laid it on one side.

When the stone was pulled up, there appeared a staircase about three or four feet deep, leading to a door. "Descend, my son," said the African magician, "those steps, and open that door. It will lead you into a palace, divided into three great halls. In each of these you will see four large brass cisterns placed on each side, full of gold and silver; but take care you do not meddle with them. Before you enter the first hall, be sure to tuck up your robe, wrap it about you, and then pass through the second into the third without stopping. Above all things, have a care that you do not touch the walls so much as with your clothes; for if you do you will die instantly. At the end of the third hall, you will find a door which opens into a garden, planted with fine trees loaded with fruit. Walk directly across the garden to a terrace, where you will see a niche before you, and in that niche a lighted lamp. Take the lamp down and put it out. When you have thrown away the wick and poured out the liquor, put it in your waistband and bring it to me. Do not be afraid that the liquor will spoil your clothes, for it is not oil, and the lamp will be dry as soon as it is thrown out."

After these words the magician drew a ring off his finger, and put it on one of Aladdin's, saying: "It is a talisman against all evil as long as you obey me. Go, therefore, boldly, and we shall both be rich all our lives."

Aladdin descended the steps, and opening the door, found the three halls just as the African magician had described. He went through them with all the precaution the fear of death could inspire, crossed the garden without stopping, took down the lamp from the niche, threw out the wick and the liquor, and, as the magician had desired, put it in his waistband. But as he came down from the terrace, seeing it was perfectly dry, he stopped in the garden to observe the trees, which were loaded with extraordinary fruit of different colours on each tree. Some bore fruit entirely white, and some clear and transparent as crystal; some pale red, and others deeper; some green, blue, and purple, and others yellow; in short, there was fruit of all colours. The white were pearls; the clear and transparent, diamonds; the deep red, rubies; the paler, balas rubies; the green, emeralds; the blue, turquoises; the purple, amethysts; and the yellow, sapphires. Aladdin, ignorant of their value, would have preferred figs, or grapes, or pomegranates; but as he had his uncle's permission, he resolved to gather some of every sort. Having filled the two new purses his uncle had bought for him with his clothes, he wrapped some up in the skirts of his vest, and crammed his bosom as full as it could hold.

Aladdin, having thus loaded himself with riches of which he knew not the value, returned through the three halls with the utmost precaution, and soon arrived at the mouth of the cave, where the African magician awaited him with the utmost impatience. As soon as Aladdin saw him, he cried out: "Pray, uncle, lend me your hand, to help me out." "Give me the lamp first," replied the magician; "it will be troublesome to you." "Indeed, uncle," answered Aladdin, "I cannot now, but I will as soon as I am up." The African magician was determined that he would have the lamp before he would help him up; and Aladdin, who had encumbered himself so much with his fruit that he could not well get at it, refused to give it to him till he was out of the cave. The African magician, provoked at this obstinate refusal, flew into a passion, threw a little of his incense into the fire, and pronounced two magical words, when the stone which had closed the mouth of the staircase moved into its place, with the earth over it in the same manner as it lay at the arrival of the magician and Aladdin.

This action of the magician plainly revealed to Aladdin that he was no uncle of his, but one who designed him evil. The truth was that he had learnt from his magic books the secret and the value of this wonderful lamp, the owner of which would be made richer than any earthly ruler, and hence his journey to China. His art had also told him that he was not permitted to take it himself, but must receive it as a voluntary gift from the hands of another person. Hence he employed young Aladdin, and hoped by a mixture of kindness and authority to make him obedient to his word and will. When he found that his attempt had failed, he set out to return to Africa, but avoided the town, lest any person who had seen him leave in company with Aladdin should make inquiries after the youth. Aladdin being suddenly enveloped in darkness, cried, and called out to his uncle to tell him he was ready to give him the lamp; but in vain, since his cries could not be heard. He descended to the bottom of the steps, with a design to get into the palace, but the door, which was opened before by enchantment, was now shut by the same means. He then redoubled his cries and tears, and sat down on the steps without any hopes of ever seeing light again, and in an expectation of passing from the present darkness to a speedy death. In this great emergency he said: "There is no strength or power but in the great and high God"; and in joining his hands to pray he rubbed the ring which the magician had put on his finger. Immediately a genie of frightful aspect appeared, and said: "What wouldst thou have? I am ready to obey thee. I serve him who possesses the ring on thy finger; I and the other slaves of that ring."

At another time Aladdin would have been frightened at the sight of so extraordinary a figure, but the danger he was in made him answer without hesitation: "Whoever thou art, deliver me from this place." He had no sooner spoken these words, than he found himself on the very spot where the magician had last left him, and no sign of cave nor opening nor disturbance of the earth. Returning God thanks to find himself once more in the world, he made the best of his way home. When he got within his mother's door, the joy to see her and his weakness for want of sustenance made him so faint that he remained for a long time as dead. As soon as he recovered, he related to his mother all that had happened to him, and they were both very vehement in their complaints of the cruel magician. Aladdin slept very soundly till late the next morning, when the first thing he said to his mother was that he wanted something to eat, and wished she would give him his breakfast. "Alas! child," said she, "I have not a bit of bread to give you. You ate up all the provisions I had in the house yesterday; but I have a little cotton which I have spun; I will go and sell it, and buy bread and something for our dinner." "Mother," replied Aladdin, "keep your cotton for another time, and give me the lamp I brought home with me yesterday; I will go and sell it, and the money I shall get for it will serve both for breakfast and dinner, and perhaps supper, too."

Aladdin's mother took the lamp and said to her son: "Here it is, but it is very dirty; if it were a little cleaner I believe it would bring something more." She took some fine sand and water to clean it; but had no sooner begun to rub it, than in an instant a hideous genie of gigantic size appeared before her, and said to her in a voice of thunder: "What wouldst thou have? I am ready to obey thee as thy slave, and the slave of all those who have that lamp in their hands; I and the other slaves of the lamp."

Aladdin's mother, terrified at the sight of the genie, fainted; when Aladdin, who had seen such a phantom in the cavern, snatched the lamp out of his mother's hand and said to the genie boldly; "I am hungry, bring me something to eat." The genie disappeared immediately, and in an instant returned with a large silver tray, holding twelve covered dishes of the same metal, which contained the most delicious viands; six large white bread cakes on two plates, two flagons of wine, and two silver cups. All these he placed upon a carpet and disappeared; this was done before Aladdin's mother recovered from her swoon.

Aladdin had fetched some water, and sprinkled it in her face to recover her. Whether that or the smell of the meat effected her cure, it was not long before she came to herself. "Mother," said Aladdin, "be not afraid: get up and eat; here is what will put you in heart, and at the same time satisfy my extreme hunger."

His mother was much surprised to see the great tray, twelve dishes, six loaves, the two flagons and cups, and to smell the savoury odour which exhaled from the dishes. "Child," said she, "to whom are we obliged for this great plenty and liberality? Has the sultan been made acquainted with our poverty and had compassion on us?" "It is no matter, mother," said

Aladdin, "let us sit down and eat; for you have almost as much need of a good breakfast as myself; when we have done, I will tell you." Accordingly, both mother and son sat down and ate with the better relish as the table was so well furnished. But all the time Aladdin's mother could not forbear looking at and admiring the tray and dishes, though she could not judge whether they were silver or any other metal, and the novelty more than the value attracted her attention.

The mother and son sat at breakfast till it was dinner time, and then they thought it would be best to put the two meals together; yet, after this they found they should have enough left for supper, and two meals for the next day.

When Aladdin's mother had taken away and set by what was left, she went and sat down by her son on the sofa, saying: "I expect now that you should satisfy my impatience, and tell me exactly what passed between the genie and you while I was in a swoon"; which he readily complied with.

She was in as great amazement at what her son told her, as at the appearance of the genie; and said to him: "But, son, what have we to do with genii? I never heard that any of my acquaintance had ever seen one. How came that vile genie to address himself to me, and not to you, to whom he had appeared before in the cave?" "Mother," answered Aladdin, "the genie you

saw is not the one who appeared to me. If you remember, he that I first saw called himself the slave of
the ring on my finger; and this you saw, called himself
the slave of the lamp you had in your hand; but I
believe you did not hear him, for I think you fainted as
soon as he began to speak."

"What!" cried the mother, "was your lamp then the
occasion of that cursed genie's addressing himself rather
to me than to you? Ah! my son, take it out of my sight,
and put it where you please. I had rather you would
sell it than run the hazard of being frightened to death
again by touching it, and if you would take my advice,
you would part also with the ring, and not have anything to do with genii, who, as our prophet has told
us, are only devils."

"With your leave, mother," replied Aladdin, "I shall
now take care how I sell a lamp which may be so serviceable to both you and me. That false and wicked
magician would not have undertaken so long a journey
to secure this wonderful lamp if he had not known its
value to exceed that of gold and silver. And since
we have honestly come by it, let us make a profitable use
of it, without making any great show and exciting the
envy and jealousy of our neighbours. However, since
the genii frighten you so much, I will take it out of your
sight, and put it where I may find it when I want it. The
ring I cannot resolve to part with; for without that you

had never seen me again, and though I am alive now, perhaps if it were gone, I might not be so some moments hence; therefore, I hope you will give me leave to keep it, and to wear it always on my finger." Aladdin's mother replied that he might do what he pleased; for her part, she would have nothing to do with genii, and never say anything more about them.

By the next night they had eaten all the provisions the genie had brought; and the next day Aladdin, who could not bear the thoughts of hunger, putting one of the silver dishes under his vest, went out early to sell it, and addressing himself to a Jew whom he met in the streets, took him aside, and pulling out the plate asked him if he would buy it. The cunning Jew took the dish, examined it, and as soon as he found that it was good silver, asked Aladdin at how much he valued it. Aladdin, who had never been used to such traffic, told him he would trust to his judgment and honour. The Jew was somewhat confounded at this plain dealing, and doubting whether Aladdin understood the material or the full value of what he offered to sell, took a piece of gold out of his purse and gave it him, though it was but the sixtieth part of the worth of the plate. Aladdin, taking the money very eagerly, retired with so much haste, that the Jew, not content with the exorbitancy of his profit, was vexed he had not penetrated into his ignorance, and was going to run after him, to endeavour to get some change out of the piece of gold; but he ran so fast, and had got so far, that it would have been impossible for him to overtake him.

Before Aladdin went home, he called at a baker's, bought some cakes of bread, changed his money, and on his return gave the rest to his mother, who went and purchased provisions enough to last them some time. After this manner they lived, till Aladdin had sold the twelve dishes singly, as necessity pressed, to the Jew for the same money; who, after the first time, durst not offer him less for fear of losing so good a bargain. When he had sold the last dish, he had recourse to the tray, which weighed ten times as much as the dishes, and would have carried it to his old purchaser, but that it was too large and cumbersome; therefore he was obliged to bring him home with him to his mother's, where, after the Jew had examined the weight of the tray, he laid down ten pieces of gold, with which Aladdin was very well satisfied.

When all the money was spent, Aladdin had recourse again to the lamp. He took it in his hands, looked for the part where his mother had rubbed it with the sand, rubbed it also, when the genie immediately appeared, and said: "What wouldst thou have? I am ready to obey thee as thy slave, and the slave of all those who have that lamp in their hands; I and the other slaves of the lamp." "I am hungry," said Aladdin, "bring me something to eat." The genie disappeared, and presently returned with a tray, the same number of covered dishes as before, set them down, and vanished.

As soon as Aladdin found that their provisions were again expended, he took one of the dishes, and went to look for his Jew chapman; but passing by a goldsmith's shop, the goldsmith perceiving him, called to him, and said: "My lad, I imagine that you have something to sell to the Jew, whom I often see you visit; but perhaps you do not know that he is the greatest rogue even among the Jews. I will give you the full worth of what you have to sell, or I will direct you to other merchants who will not cheat you."

This offer induced Aladdin to pull his plate from under his vest and show it to the goldsmith, who at first sight saw that it was made of the finest silver, and asked him if he had sold such as that to the Jew; when Aladdin told him that he had sold him twelve such for a piece of gold each. "What a villain!" cried the goldsmith. "But," added he, "my son, what is past cannot be re-called. By showing you the value of this plate, which is of the finest silver we use in our shops, I will let you see how much the Jew has cheated you."

The goldsmith took a pair of scales, weighed the dish, and assured him that his plate would fetch by weight sixty pieces of gold, which he offered to pay down immediately.

Aladdin thanked him for his fair dealing, and never after went to any other person.

Though Aladdin and his mother had an inexhaustible treasure in their lamp, and might have had whatever they wished for, yet they lived with the same frugality as before, and it may easily be supposed that the money for which Aladdin had sold the dishes and tray was sufficient to maintain them some time.

During this interval, Aladdin frequented the shops of the principal merchants, where they sold cloth of gold and silver, linens, silk stuffs, and jewellery, and oftentimes joining in their conversation, acquired a knowledge of the world and a desire to improve himself. By his acquaintance among the jewellers, he came to know that the fruits which he had gathered when he took the lamp were, instead of coloured glass, stones of inestimable value, but he had prudence not to mention this to any one, not even to his mother.

One day as Aladdin was walking about the town, he heard an order proclaimed, commanding the people to shut up their shops and houses and keep within doors while the Princess Buddir al Buddoor, the sultan's daughter, went to the bath and returned.

This proclamation inspired Aladdin with eager desire to see the princess's face, which he determined to gratify by placing himself behind the door of the bath so that he could not fail to see her face.

ALADDIN; OR, THE WONDERFUL LAMP

Aladdin had not long concealed himself before the princess came. She was attended by a great crowd of ladies, slaves, and mutes, who walked on each side and behind her. When she came within three or four paces of the door of the bath she took off her veil and gave Aladdin an opportunity of a full view at her face.

The princess was a noted beauty; her eyes were large, lively, and sparkling; her smile bewitching; her nose faultless; her mouth small; her lips vermilion. It is not therefore surprising that Aladdin, who had never before seen such a blaze of charms, was dazzled and enchanted.

After the princess had passed by and entered the bath, Aladdin quitted his hiding-place and went home. His mother perceived him to be more thoughtful and melancholy than usual, and asked what had happened to make him so, or if he was ill. He then told his mother all his adventure, and concluded by declaring: "I love the princess more than I can express, and am resolved that I will ask her in marriage of the sultan."

Aladdin's mother listened with surprise to what her son told her; but when he talked of asking the princess in marriage, she laughed aloud. "Alas! child," said she, "what are you thinking of? You must be mad to talk thus."

"I assure you, mother," replied Aladdin, "that I am not mad, but in my right senses. I foresaw that you would reproach me with folly and extravagance; but I must tell you once more, that I am resolved to demand the princess of the sultan in marriage, nor do I despair of success. I have the slaves of the lamp and of the ring to help me, and you know how powerful their aid is. And I have another secret to tell you: those pieces of glass, which I got from the trees in the garden of the subterranean palace, are jewels of inestimable value, and fit for the greatest monarchs. All the precious stones the jewellers have in Bagdad are not to be compared to mine for size or beauty; and I am sure that the offer of them will secure the favour of the sultan. You have a large porcelain dish fit to hold them; fetch it, and let us see how they will look when we have arranged them according to their different colours."

Aladdin's mother brought the china dish, when he took the jewels out of the two purses in which he had kept them, and placed them in order, according to his fancy. But the brightness and lustre they emitted in the daytime, and the variety of the colours, so dazzled the eyes of both mother and son that they were astonished beyond measure. Aladdin's mother, emboldened by the sight of these rich jewels, and fearful lest her son be guilty of greater extravagance, complied with his request, and promised to go early the next morning to the palace of the sultan. Aladdin rose before daybreak, awakened his mother, pressing her to go to the sultan's palace, and to get admittance, if possible, before the grand vizier, the other viziers, and the great officers of state went in to take their seats in the divan where the sultan always attended in person.

Aladdin's mother took the china dish in which they had put the jewels the day before, wrapped it in two fine napkins, and set forward for the sultan's palace. When she came to the gates, the grand vizier, the other viziers, and most distinguished lords of the court were just gone in; but notwithstanding the crowd of people was great, she got into the divan, a spacious hall, the entrance into which was very magnificent. She placed herself just before the sultan, grand vizier, and the great lords who sat in council on his right and his left hand. Several causes were called, according to their order, pleaded and adjudged, until the time the divan generally broke up, when the sultan, rising, returned to his apartment, attended by the grand vizier; the other viziers and ministers of state then retired, as also did all those whose business had called them thither.

Aladdin's mother, seeing the sultan retire and all the people depart, judged rightly that he would not sit again that day, and resolved to go home; and on her arrival said, with much simplicity: "Son, I have seen the sultan, and am very well persuaded he has seen me, too, for I placed myself just before him; but he was so much taken up with those who attended on all sides of him that I pitied him, and wondered at his patience. At last I believe he was heartily tired, for he rose up suddenly and would not hear a great many who were ready prepared to speak to him, but went away, at which I was well pleased, for indeed I began to lose all patience, and was extremely fatigued by staying so long. But there is no harm done; I will go again to-morrow; perhaps the sultan may not be so busy."

The next morning she repaired to the sultan's palace with the present, as early as the day before; but when she came there, she found the gates of the divan shut. She went six times afterward on the days appointed, placed herself always directly before the sultan, but with as little success as the first morning.

On the sixth day, however, after the divan was broken up, when the sultan returned to his own apartment, he said to his grand vizier: "I have for some time observed a certain woman, who attends constantly every day that I give audience, with something wrapped up in a napkin; she always stands up from the beginning to the breaking up of the audience, and affects to place herself just before me. If this woman comes to our next audience, do not fail to call her, that I may hear what she has to say." The grand vizier made answer by lowering his hand and then lifting it up above his head, signifying his willingness to lose it if he failed.

On the next audience day, when Aladdin's mother

went to the divan and placed herself in front of the sultan, as usual, the grand vizier immediately called the chief of the mace-bearers, and pointing to her bade him bring her before the sultan. The old woman at once followed the mace-bearer, and when she reached the sultan, bowed her head down to the carpet which covered the platform of the throne, and remained in that posture until he bade her rise, which she had no sooner done than he said to her: "Good woman, I have observed you to stand many days from the beginning to the rising of the divan; what business brings you here?"

After these words, Aladdin's mother prostrated herself a second time; and when she arose, said: "Monarch of monarchs, I beg of you to pardon the boldness of my petition, and to assure me of your pardon and forgiveness." "Well," replied the sultan, "I will forgive you be it what it may, and no hurt shall come to you; speak boldly."

When Aladdin's mother had taken all these precautions for fear of the sultan's anger, she told him faithfully the errand on which her son had sent her, and the event which led to his making so bold a request in spite of all her remonstrances.

The sultan hearkened to this discourse without showing the least anger; but before he gave her any answer, asked her what she had brought tied up in the napkin. She took the china dish which she had set down at the foot of the throne, untied it, and presented it to the sultan. The sultan's amazement and surprise were inexpressible when he saw so many large, beautiful, and valuable jewels collected in the dish. He remained for some time lost in admiration. At last, when he had recovered himself, he received the present from Aladdin's mother's hand, saying: "How rich, how beautiful!" After he had admired and handled all the jewels one after another, he turned to his grand vizier, and showing him the dish, said: "Behold, admire, wonder! and confess that your eyes never beheld jewels so rich and beautiful before." The vizier was charmed. "Well," continued the sultan, "what sayest thou to such a present? Is it not worthy of the princess, my daughter? And ought I not to bestow her on one who values her at so great a price?" "I cannot but own," replied the grand vizier, "that the present is worthy of the princess; but I beg of your Majesty to grant me three months before you come to a final resolution. I hope, before that time, my son, whom you have regarded with your favour, will be able to make a nobler present than this Aladdin, who is an entire stranger to your Majesty."

The sultan granted his request, and he said to the old woman: "Good woman, go home and tell your son that I agree to the proposal you have made me, but I cannot marry the princess my daughter for three months; at the expiration of that time come again."

ALADDIN; OR, THE WONDERFUL LAMP

Aladdin's mother returned home much more gratified than she had expected, and told her son with much joy the condescending answer she had received from the sultan's own mouth; and that she was to come to the divan again that day three months.

Aladdin thought himself the most happy of all men at hearing this news, and thanked his mother for the pains she had taken in the affair, the good success of which was of so great importance to his peace that he counted every day, week, and even hour as it passed. When two of the three months were passed, his mother one evening, having no oil in the house, went out to buy some, and found a general rejoicing—the houses dressed with foliage, silks, and carpeting, and every one striving to show their joy according to their ability. The streets were crowded with officers in habits of ceremony, mounted on horses richly caparisoned, each attended by a great many footmen. Aladdin's mother asked the oil merchant what was the meaning of all this preparation of public festivity. "Whence came you good woman," said he, "that you don't know that the grand vizier's son is to marry the Princess Buddir al Buddoor, the sultan's daughter, to-night? She will presently return from the bath; and these officers whom you see are to assist at the calvacade to the palace, where the ceremony is to be solemnised."

Aladdin's mother, on hearing the news, ran home very

quickly. "Child," cried she, "you are undone! the sultan's fine promises will come to nought. This night the grand vizier's son is to marry the Princess Buddir al Buddoor."

At this account, Aladdin was thunderstruck, and he bethought himself of the lamp, and of the genie who had promised to obey him; and without indulging in idle words against the sultan, the vizier, or his son, he determined, if possible, to prevent the marriage.

When Aladdin had got into his chamber, he took the lamp, rubbed it in the same place as before, when immediately the genie appeared and said to him: "What wouldst thou have? I am ready to obey thee as thy slave; I and the other slaves of the lamp." "Hear me," said Aladdin; "thou hast hitherto obeyed me, but now I am about to impose on thee a harder task. The sultan's daughter, who was promised me as my bride, is this night married to the son of the grand vizier. Bring them both hither to me immediately they retire to their bedchamber."

"Master," replied the genie, "I obey you."

Aladdin supped with his mother as was their wont, and then went to his own apartment, and sat up to await the return of the genie, according to his commands.

In the meantime the festivities in honour of the princess's marriage were conducted in the sultan's palace with great magnificence. The ceremonies were at last brought to a conclusion, and the princess and the son of the vizier retired to the bedchamber prepared for them. No sooner had they entered it and dismissed their attendants, than the genie, the faithful slave of the lamp, to the great amazement and alarm of the bride and bridegroom, took up the bed and, by an agency invisible to them, transported it in an instant into Aladdin's chamber, where he set it down. "Remove the bridegroom," said Aladdin to the genie, "and keep him a prisoner till to-morrow dawn, and then return with him here." On Aladdin being left alone with the princess, he endeavoured to assuage her fears, and explained to her the treachery practised upon him by the sultan, her father. He then laid himself down beside her, putting a drawn scimitar between them to show that he was determined to secure her safety and to treat her with the utmost possible respect. At break of day, the genie appeared at the appointed hour, bringing back the bridegroom, whom by breathing upon he had left motionless and entranced at the door of Aladdin's chamber during the night, and at Aladdin's command transported the couch with the bride and bridegroom on it, by the same invisible agency, into the palace of the sultan.

At the instant that the genie had set down the couch with the bride and bridegroom in their own chamber, the sultan came to the door to offer his good wishes to his daughter. The grand vizier's son, who was almost perished with cold by standing in his thin undergarment all night, no sooner heard the knocking at the door, than he got out of bed and ran into the robing-chamber where he had undressed himself the night before.

The sultan having opened the door, went to the bedside, kissed the princess on the forehead, but was extremely surprised to see her look so melancholy. She only cast at him a sorrowful look, expressive of great affliction. He suspected there was something extraordinary in this silence, and thereupon went immediately to the sultaness's apartment, told her in what a state he found the princess and how she had received him. "Sire," said the sultaness, "I will go and see her; she will not receive me in the same manner."

The princess received her mother with sighs and tears and signs of deep dejection. At last, upon her pressing on her the duty of telling her all her thoughts, she gave to the sultaness a precise description of all that had happened to her during the night; on which the sultaness enjoined on her the necessity of silence and discretion, as no one would give credence to so strange a tale. The grand vizier's son, elated with the honour of being the sultan's son-in-law, kept silence on his part, and the events of the night were not allowed to cast the least gloom on the festivities on the following day, in continued celebration of the royal marriage.

When night came, the bride and bridegroom were

again attended to their chamber with the same ceremonies as on the preceding evening. Aladdin, knowing
that this would be so, had already given his commands to the genie of the lamp; and no sooner were
they alone, than their bed was removed in the same mysterious manner as on the preceding evening; and having
passed the night in the same unpleasant way, they were
in the morning conveyed to the palace of the sultan.
Scarcely had they been replaced in their apartment,
when the sultan came to make his compliments to his
daughter, when the princess could no longer conceal
from him the unhappy treatment she had been subject
to, and told him all that had happened as she had already
related it to her mother. The sultan, on hearing these
strange tidings, consulted with the grand vizier; and
finding from him that his son had been subjected to even
worse treatment by an invisible agency, he determined
to declare the marriage to be cancelled, and all the festivities, which were yet to last for several days, to be
countermanded and terminated.

This sudden change in the mind of the sultan gave
rise to various speculations and reports. Nobody but
Aladdin knew the secret, and he kept it with the most
scrupulous silence; and neither the sultan nor the grand
vizier, who had forgotten Aladdin and his request, had
the least thought that he had any hand in the strange
adventures that befell the bride and bridegroom.

On the very day that the three months contained in the sultan's promise expired, the mother of Aladdin again went to the palace and stood in the same place in the divan. The sultan knew her again, and directed his vizier to have her brought before him.

After having prostrated herself, she made answer, in reply to the sultan: "Sire, I come at the end of three months to ask of you the fulfilment of the promise you made to my son." The sultan little thought the request of Aladdin's mother was made to him in earnest, or that he would hear any more of the matter. He therefore took counsel with his vizier, who suggested that the sultan should attach such conditions to the marriage that no one of the humble condition of Aladdin could possibly fulfill. In accordance with this suggestion of the vizier, the sultan replied to the mother of Aladdin: "Good woman, it is true sultans ought to abide by their word, and I am ready to keep mine by making your son happy in marriage with the princess, my daughter. But as I cannot marry her without some further proof of your son being able to support her in royal state, you may tell him I will fulfill my promise as soon as he shall send me forty trays of massy gold, full of the same sort of jewels you have already made me a present of, and carried by a like number of black slaves, who shall be led by as many young and handsome white slaves, all dressed magnificently. On these conditions I am ready to bestow the princess, my daughter, upon him; therefore, good woman, go and tell him so, and I will wait till you bring me his answer."

Aladdin's mother prostrated herself a second time before the sultan's throne, and retired. On her way home, she laughed within herself at her son's foolish imagination. "Where," said she, "can he get so many large gold trays and such precious stones to fill them? It is altogether out of his power, and I believe he will not be much pleased with my embassy this time." When she came home, full of these thoughts, she told Aladdin all the circumstances of her interview with the sultan, and the conditions on which he consented to the marriage. "The sultan expects your answer immediately," said she; and then added, laughing: "I believe he may wait long enough!"

"Not so long, mother, as you imagine," replied Aladdin. "This demand is a mere trifle, and will prove no bar to my marriage with the princess. I will prepare at once to satisfy his request."

Aladdin retired to his own apartment and summoned the genie of the lamp, and required him to prepare and present the gift immediately, before the sultan closed his morning audience, according to the terms in which it had been prescribed. The genie professed his obedience to the owner of the lamp, and disappeared. Within a very short time, a train of forty black slaves, led by the same number of white slaves, appeared opposite the house in which Aladdin lived. Each black slave carried on his head a basin of massy gold, full of pearls, diamonds, rubies, and emeralds. Aladdin then addressed his mother: "Madam, pray lose no time; before the sultan and the divan rise, I would have you return to the palace with this present as the dowry demanded for the princess, that he may judge by my diligence and exactness of the ardent and sincere desire I have to procure myself the honour of this alliance."

As soon as this magnificent procession, with Aladdin's mother at its head, had begun to march from Aladdin's house, the whole city was filled with crowds of people desirous to see so grand a sight. The graceful bearing, elegant form, and wonderful likeness of each slave; their grave walk at an equal distance from each other; the lustre of their jewelled girdles, and the brilliancy of the aigrettes of precious stones in their turbans; all excited the greatest admiration in the spectators. As they had to pass through several streets to the palace, the whole length of the way was lined with files of spectators. Nothing, indeed, was ever seen so beautiful and brilliant in the sultan's palace, and the richest robes of the emirs of his court were not to be compared to the costly dresses of these slaves, whom they supposed to be kings.

As the sultan, who had been informed of their approach, had given orders for them to be admitted, they met with no obstacle, but went into the divan in regular order, one part turning to the right and the other to the left. After they were all entered and had formed a semicircle before the sultan's throne, the black slaves laid the golden trays on the carpet, prostrated themselves, touching the carpet with their foreheads, and at the same time the white slaves did the same. When they rose, the black slaves uncovered the trays, and then all stood with their arms crossed over their breasts.

In the meantime, Aladdin's mother advanced to the foot of the throne, and having prostrated herself, said to the sultan: "Sire, my son knows this present is much below the notice of Princess Buddir al Buddoor; but hopes, nevertheless, that your Majesty will accept of it and make it agreeable to the princess, and with the greater confidence since he has endeavoured to conform to the conditions you were pleased to impose."

The sultan, overpowered at the sight of such more than royal magnificence, replied without hesitation to the words of Aladdin's mother: "Go and tell your son that I wait with open arms to embrace him; and the more haste he makes to come and receive the princess, my daughter, from my hands, the greater pleasure he will do me." As soon as Aladdin's mother had retired, the sultan put an end to the audience; and, rising from his throne, ordered that the princess's attendants should come and carry the trays into their mistress's apartment, whither he went himself to examine them with her at his leisure. The fourscore slaves were conducted into the palace; and the sultan, telling the princess of their magnificent apparel, ordered them to be brought before her apartment, that she might see through the lattices he had not exaggerated in his account of them.

In the meantime Aladdin's mother reached home, and showed in her air and countenance the good news she brought to her son. "My son," said she, "you may rejoice you are arrived at the height of your desires. The sultan has declared that you shall marry the Princess Buddir al Buddoor. He waits for you with impatience."

Aladdin, enraptured with this news, made his mother very little reply, but retired to his chamber. There he rubbed his lamp, and the obedient genie appeared. "Genie," said Aladdin, "convey me at once to a bath and supply me with the richest and most magnificent robe ever worn by a monarch." No sooner were the words out of his mouth than the genie rendered him, as well as himself, invisible, and transported him into a bath of the finest marble of all sorts of colours, where he was undressed, without seeing by whom, in a magnificent and spacious hall. He was then well rubbed and washed with various scented waters. After he had passed through several degrees of heat, he came out quite a different man from what he was before. His skin was clear as that of a child, his body lightsome and free; and when he returned into the hall, he found, instead of his own poor raiment, a robe, the magnificence of which astonished him. The genie helped him to dress, and when he had done, transported him back to his own chamber, where he asked him if he had any other commands. "Yes," answered Aladdin, "bring me a charger that surpasses in beauty and goodness the best in the sultan's stables, with a saddle, bridle, and other caparisons to correspond with his value. Furnish also twenty slaves, as richly clothed as those who carried the present to the sultan, to walk by my side and follow me, and twenty more to go before me in two ranks. Besides these, bring my mother six women slaves to attend her, as richly dressed at least as any of the Princess Buddir al Buddoor's, each carrying a complete dress fit for any sultaness. I want also ten thousand pieces of gold in ten purses; go, and make haste."

As soon as Aladdin had given these orders, the genie disappeared, but presently returned with the horse, the forty slaves, ten of whom carried each a purse containing ten thousand pieces of gold, and six women slaves, each carrying on her head a different dress for Aladdin's mother, wrapt up in a piece of silver tissue, and presented them all to Aladdin.

He presented the six women slaves to his mother, telling her they were her slaves, and that the dresses they had brought were for her use. Of the ten purses

235

Aladdin took four, which he gave to his mother, telling her those were to supply her with necessaries; the other six he left in the hands of the slaves who brought them, with an order to throw them by handfuls among the people as they went to the sultan's palace. The six slaves who carried the purses he ordered likewise to march before him, three on the right hand and three on the left.

When Aladdin had thus prepared himself for his first interview with the sultan, he dismissed the genie, and immediately mounting his charger, began his march, and though he never was on horseback before, appeared with a grace the most experienced horseman might envy. The innumerable concourse of people through whom he passed made the air echo with their acclamations, especially every time the six slaves who carried the purses threw handfuls of gold among the populace.

On Aladdin's arrival at the palace, the sultan was surprised to find him more richly and magnificently robed than he had ever been himself, and was impressed with his good looks and dignity of manner, which were so different from what he expected in the son of one so humble as Aladdin's mother. He embraced him with all the demonstrations of joy, and when he would have fallen at his feet, held him by the hand and made him sit near his throne. He shortly after led him, amidst the sounds of trumpets, hautboys, and all kinds of music, to a magnificent entertainment, at which the sultan and Aladdin ate by themselves, and the great lords of the court, according to their rank and dignity, sat at different tables. After the feast, the sultan sent for the chief cadi, and commanded him to draw up a contract of marriage between the Princess Buddir al Buddoor and Aladdin. When the contract had been drawn, the sultan asked Aladdin if he would stay in the palace and complete the ceremonies of the marriage that day. "Sire," said Aladdin, "though great is my impatience to enter on the honour granted me by your Majesty, yet I beg you to permit me first to build a palace worthy to receive the princess your daughter. I pray you to grant me sufficient ground near your palace, and I will have it completed with the utmost expedition." The sultan granted Aladdin his request, and again embraced him. After which he took his leave with as much politeness as if he had been bred up and had always lived at court.

Aladdin returned home in the order he had come, amidst the acclamations of the people, who wished him all happiness and prosperity. As soon as he dismounted, he retired to his own chamber, took the lamp, and summoned the genie as usual, who professed his allegiance. "Genie," said Aladdin, "build me a palace fit to receive the Princess Buddir al Buddoor. Let its materials be made of nothing less than porphyry, jasper, agate, lapis lazuli, and the finest marble. Let its walls be massive gold and silver bricks laid alternately. Let each front contain six windows, and let the lattices of these (except one, which must be left unfinished) be enriched with diamonds, rubies, and emeralds, so that they shall exceed everything of the kind ever seen in the world. Let there be an inner and outer court in front of the palace, and a spacious garden; but, above all things, provide a safe treasure-house and fill it with gold and silver. Let there be also kitchens and storehouses, stables full of the finest horses, with their equerries and grooms, and hunting equipage, officers, attendants, and slaves, both men and women, to form a retinue for the princess and myself. Go and execute my wishes."

When Aladdin gave these commands to the genie, the sun was set. The next morning at daybreak the genie presented himself, and having obtained Aladdin's consent, transported him in a moment to the palace he had made. The genie led him through all the apartments, where he found officers and slaves, habited according to their rank and the services to which they were appointed. The genie then showed him the treasury, which was opened by a treasurer, where Aladdin saw large vases of different sizes, piled up to the top with money, ranged all round the chamber. The genie thence led him to the stables, where were some of the finest horses in the world, and the grooms busy in dressing them; from thence they went to the storehouses, which were filled with all things necessary, both for food and ornament.

When Aladdin had examined every portion of the palace, and particularly the hall with the four-and-twenty windows, and found it far to exceed his fondest expectations, he said: "Genie, there is one thing wanting: a fine carpet for the princess to walk upon from the sultan's palace to mine. Lay one down immediately." The genie disappeared, and Aladdin saw what he desired executed in an instant. The genie then returned, and carried him to his own home.

When the sultan's porters came to open the gates, they were amazed to find what had been an unoccupied garden filled up with a magnificent palace, and a splendid carpet extending to it all the way from the sultan's palace. They told the strange tidings to the grand vizier, who informed the sultan, who exclaimed: "It must be Aladdin's palace, which I gave him leave to build for my daughter. He has wished to surprise us, and let us see what wonders can be done in only one night."

Aladdin, on his being conveyed by the genie to his own home, requested his mother to go to the Princess Buddir al Buddoor, and tell her that the palace would be ready for her reception in the evening. She went, attended by her women slaves, in the same order as on the preceding day. Shortly after her arrival at the princess's apartment, the sultan himself came in, and was surprised to find her, whom he knew as his suppliant at his divan in such humble guise, to be now more richly and sumptuously attired than his own daughter. This gave him a higher opinion of Aladdin, who took such care of his mother and made her share his wealth and honours. Shortly after her departure, Aladdin, mounting his horse and attended by his retinue of magnificent attendants, left his paternal home forever, and went to the palace in the same pomp as on the day before. Nor did he forget to take with him the Wonderful Lamp, to which he owed all his good fortune, nor to wear the Ring which was given him as a talisman. The sultan entertained Aladdin with the utmost magnificence, and at night, on the conclusion of the marriage ceremonies, the princess took leave of the sultan, her father. Bands of music led the procession, followed by a hundred state ushers, and the like number of black mutes in two files, with their officers at their head. Four hundred of the sultan's young pages carried flambeaux on each side, which, together with the illuminations of the sultan's and Aladdin's palaces, made it as light as day. In this order the princess, conveyed in her litter, and accompanied also by Aladdin's mother, carried in a superb litter and attended by her women slaves, proceeded on the carpet which was spread from the sultan's palace to that of Aladdin. On her arrival Aladdin was ready to receive her at the entrance, and led her into a large hall, illuminated with an infinite number of wax candles, where a noble feast was served up. The dishes were of massy gold, and contained the most delicate viands. The vases, basins, and goblets were gold also and of exquisite workmanship, and all the other ornaments and embellishments of the hall were answerable to this display. The princess, dazzled to see so much riches collected in one place, said to Aladdin: "I thought, prince, that nothing in the world was so beautiful as the sultan's, my father's, palace, but the sight of this hall alone is sufficient to show I was deceived."

When the supper was ended, there entered a company of female dancers, who performed according to the custom of the country, singing at the same time verses in praise of the bride and bridegroom. About midnight Aladdin's mother conducted the bride to the nuptial apartment, and he soon after retired.

The next morning the attendants of Aladdin presented themselves to dress him, and brought him another habit, as rich and magnificent as that worn the day before. He then ordered one of the horses to be got ready, mounted him, and went in the midst of a large troop of slaves to the sultan's palace to entreat him to take a repast in the princess's palace, attended by his grand vizier and all the lords of his court. The sultan consented with pleasure, rose up immediately, and, preceded by the principal officers of his palace and followed by all the great lords of his court, accompanied Aladdin.

The nearer the sultan approached Aladdin's palace, the more he was struck with its beauty; but when he entered it, came into the hall, and saw the windows enriched with diamonds, rubies, emeralds—all large perfect stones—he was completely surprised, and said to his son-in-law: "This palace is one of the wonders of the world; for where in all the world besides shall we find walls built of massy gold and silver, and diamonds, rubies, and emeralds composing the windows? But what most surprises me is that a hall of this magnificence should be left with one of its windows incomplete and unfinished." "Sire," answered Aladdin, "the omission was by design, since I wished that you should have the glory of finishing this hall." "I take your intention kindly," said the sultan, "and will give orders about it immediately."

After the sultan had finished this magnificent entertainment, provided for him and for his court by Aladdin, he was informed that the jewellers and goldsmiths attended; upon which he returned to the hall, and showed them the window which was unfinished. "I sent for you," said he, "to fit up this window in as great perfection as the rest. Examine them well, and make all the dispatch you can."

The jewellers and goldsmiths examined the three-and-twenty windows with great attention, and after they had consulted together to know what each could furnish, they returned and presented themselves before the sultan, whose principal jeweller, undertaking to speak for the rest, said: "Sire, we are all willing to exert our utmost care and industry to obey you; but among us all we cannot furnish jewels enough for so great a work." "I have more than are necessary," said the sultan; "come to my palace, and you shall choose what may answer your purpose."

When the sultan returned to his palace, he ordered his jewels to be brought out, and the jewellers took a great quantity, particularly those Aladdin had made him a present of, which they soon used, without making any great advance in their work. They came again several times for more, and in a month's time had not finished half their work. In short, they used all the jewels the sultan had, and borrowed of the vizier, but yet the work was not half done.

Aladdin, who knew that all the sultan's endeavours to make this window like the rest were in vain, sent for the jewellers and goldsmiths, and not only commanded them to desist from their work, but ordered them to undo what they had begun, and to carry all their jewels back to the sultan and to the vizier. They undid in a few hours what they had been six weeks about, and retired, leaving Aladdin alone in the hall. He took the lamp, which he carried about him, rubbed it, and presently the genie appeared. "Genie," said Aladdin, "I ordered thee to leave one of the four-and-twenty windows of this hall imperfect, and thou has executed my commands punctually; now I would have thee make it like the rest." The genie immediately disappeared. Aladdin went out of the hall, and returning soon after, found the window, as he wished it to be, like the others.

In the meantime, the jewellers and goldsmiths repaired to the palace and were introduced into the sultan's presence, where the chief jeweller presented the precious stones which he had brought back. The sultan asked them if Aladdin had given them any reason for so doing, and they answering that he had given them none, he ordered a horse to be brought, which he mounted and rode to his son-in-law's palace, with some few attendants on foot, to inquire why he had ordered the completion of the window to be stopped. Aladdin met him at the gate, and without giving any reply to his inquiries conducted him to the grand salon, where the sultan, to his great surprise, found the window, which was left imperfect, to correspond exactly with the others. He fancied at first that he was mistaken, and examined the two windows on each side, and afterward all the four-and-twenty; but when he was convinced that the window which several workmen had been so long about was finished in so short a time, he embraced Aladdin and kissed him between his eyes. "My son," said he, "what a man you are to do such surprising things always in the twinkling of an eye! There is not your fellow in the world; the more I know, the more I admire you."

The sultan returned to the palace, and after this went frequently to the window to contemplate and admire the wonderful palace of the son-in-law.

Aladdin did not confine himself in his palace, but went with much state, sometimes to one mosque and sometimes to another, to prayers, or to visit the grand vizier or the principal lords of the court. Every time he went out, he caused two slaves, who walked by the side of his horse, to throw handfuls of money among the people as he passed through the streets and squares. This generosity gained him the love and blessings of the people, and it was common for them to swear by his head. Thus Aladdin, while he paid all respect to the sultan, won by his affable behaviour and liberality the affections of the people.

Aladdin had conducted himself in this manner several years, when the African magician, who had for some years dismissed him from his recollection, determined to inform himself with certainty whether he perished, as he supposed, in the subterranean cave or not. After he had resorted to a long course of magic ceremonies and had formed a horoscope by which to ascertain Aladdin's fate, what was his surprise to find the appearances to declare that Aladdin, instead of dying in the cave, had made his escape and was living in royal splendour by the aid of the genie of the wonderful lamp!

On the very next day, the magician set out and travelled with the utmost haste to the capital of China, where, on his arrival, he took up his lodgings in a khan.

He then quickly learnt about the wealth, charities, happiness, and splendid palace of Prince Aladdin. Directly he saw the wonderful fabric, he knew that none but the genii, the slaves of the lamp, could have performed such wonders, and piqued to the quick at Aladdin's high state, he returned to the khan.

On his return he had recourse to an operation of geomancy to find out where the lamp was—whether Aladdin carried it about with him, or where he left it. The result of his consultation informed him, to his great joy, that the lamp was in the palace. "Well," said he, rubbing his hands in glee, "I shall have the lamp, and I shall make Aladdin return to his original mean condition."

The next day the magician learnt from the chief superintendent of the khan where he lodged, that Aladdin had gone on a hunting expedition, which was to last for eight days, of which only three had expired.

ALADDIN; OR, THE WONDERFUL LAMP

The magician wanted to know no more. He resolved at once on his plans. He went to a coppersmith, and asked for a dozen copper lamps; the master of the shop told him he had not so many by him, but if he would have patience till the next day, he would have them ready. The magician appointed his time, and desired him to take care that they should be handsome and well polished.

The next day the magician called for the twelve lamps, paid the man his full price, put them into a basket hanging on his arm, and went directly to Aladdin's palace. As he approached, he began crying: "Who will exchange old lamps for new ones?" As he went along, a crowd of children collected, who hooted, and thought him, as did all who chanced to be passing by, a madman or a fool to offer to change new lamps for old ones.

The African magician regarded not their scoffs, hootings, or all they could say to him, but still continued crying: "Who will change old lamps for new ones?" He repeated this so often, walking backward and forward in front of the palace, that the princess, who was then in the hall with the four-and-twenty windows, hearing a man cry something, and seeing a great mob crowding about him, sent one of her women slaves to know what he cried.

The slave returned, laughing so heartily that the

princess rebuked her. "Madam," answered the slave laughing still, "who can forbear laughing, to see an old man with a basket on his arm, full of fine new lamps, asking to change them for old ones? The children and mob crowding about him, so that he can hardly stir, make all the noise they can in derision of him."

Another female slave hearing this said: "Now you speak of lamps, I know not whether the princess may have observed it, but there is an old one upon a shelf of the Prince Aladdin's robing-room, and whoever owns it will not be sorry to find a new one in its stead. If the princess chooses, she may have the pleasure of trying if this old man is so silly as to give a new lamp for an old one without taking anything for the exchange."

The princess, who knew not the value of this lamp and the interest that Aladdin had to keep it safe, entered into the pleasantry and commanded a slave to take it and make the exchange. The slave obeyed, went out of the hall, and no sooner got to the palace gates than he saw the African magician, called to him, and showing him the old lamp, said: "Give me a new lamp for this."

The magician never doubted but this was the lamp he wanted. There could be no other such in this palace, where every utensil was gold or silver. He snatched it eagerly out of the slave's hand and, thrusting it as far as he could into his breast, offered him his basket, and bade him choose which he liked best. The slave picked out one and carried it to the princess; but the change was no sooner made than the place rang with the shouts of the children, deriding the magician's folly.

The African magician stayed no longer near the palace, nor cried any more: "New lamps for old ones," but made the best of his way to his khan. His end was answered, and by his silence he got rid of the children and the mob.

As soon as he was out of sight of the two palaces, he hastened down the least-frequented streets; and having no more occasion for his lamps or basket, set all down in a spot where nobody saw him; then going down another street or two, he walked till he came to one of the city gates, and pursuing his way through the suburbs, which were very extensive, at length reached a lonely spot, where he stopped till the darkness of the night, as the most suitable time for the design he had in contemplation. When it became quite dark, he pulled the lamp out of his breast and rubbed it. At that summons the genie appeared, and said: "What wouldst thou have? I am ready to obey thee as thy slave, and the slave of all those who have that lamp in their hands; both I and the other slaves of the lamp." "I command thee," replied the magician, "to transport me immediately, and the palace which thou and the other slaves of the lamp have built in this city, with all the people in it, to Africa." The genie made no reply, but with the assistance of the other genii, the slaves of the lamp, immediately transported him and the palace, entire, to the spot whither he had been desired to convey it.

Early the next morning, when the sultan, according to custom, went to contemplate and admire Aladdin's palace, his amazement was unbounded to find that it could nowhere be seen. He could not comprehend how so large a palace, which he had seen plainly every day for some years, should vanish so soon and not leave the least remains behind. In his perplexity he ordered the grand vizier to be sent for with expedition.

The grand vizier, who, in secret, bore no good-will to Aladdin, intimated his suspicion that the palace was built by magic, and that Aladdin had made his hunting excursion an excuse for the removal of his palace with the same suddenness with which it had been erected. He induced the sultan to send a detachment of his guard and to have Aladdin seized as a prisoner of state. On his son-in-law being brought before him, he would not hear a word from him, but ordered him to be put to death. The decree caused so much discontent among the people, whose affection Aladdin had secured by his largesses and charities, that the sultan, fearful of an insurrection, was obliged to grant him his life. When Aladdin found himself at liberty, he again addressed the sultan: "Sire, I pray you to let me know the crime by

which I have thus lost the favour of thy countenance."
"Your crime!" answered the sultan, "wretched man! do
you not know it? Follow me, and I will show you."
The sultan then took Aladdin into the apartment from
whence he was wont to look at and admire his palace,
and said: "You ought to know where your palace stood;
look, mind, and tell me what has become of it." Aladdin did so and, being utterly amazed at the loss of his
palace, was speechless. At last, recovering himself, he
said: "It is true, I do not see the palace. It is vanished, but I had no concern in its removal. I beg you
to give me forty days, and if in that time I cannot restore it, I will offer my head to be disposed of at your
pleasure." "I give you the time you ask, but at the
end of the forty days, forget not to present yourself before me."

Aladdin went out of the sultan's palace in a condition
of exceeding humiliation. The lords who had courted
him in the days of his splendour now declined to have any
communication with him. For three days he wandered
about the city, exciting the wonder and compassion of
the multitude by asking everybody he met if they had
seen his palace or could tell him anything of it. On the
third day he wandered into the country, and as he was
approaching a river, he fell down the bank with so much
violence that he rubbed the ring which the magician had
given him so hard, by holding on the rock to save him-

self, that immediately the same genie appeared whom he had seen in the cave where the magician had left him. "What wouldst thou have?" said the genie, "I am ready to obey thee as thy slave, and the slave of all those that have that ring on their finger; both I and the other slaves of the ring."

Aladdin, agreeably surprised at an offer of help so little expected, replied, "Genie, show me where the palace I caused to be built now stands, or transport it back where it first stood." "Your command," answered the genie, "is not wholly in my power; I am only the slave of the ring, and not of the lamp." "I command thee, then," replied Aladdin, "by the power of the ring, to transport me to the spot where my palace stands, what part of the world soever it may be." These words were no sooner out of his mouth than the genie transported him into Africa, to the midst of a large plain, where his palace stood, at no great distance from a city, and placing him exactly under the window of the princess's apartment, left him.

Now it so happened that shortly after Aladdin had been transported by the slave of the ring to the neighbourhood of his palace, that one of the attendants of the Princess Buddir al Buddoor, looking through the window, perceived him and instantly told her mistress. The princess, who could not believe the joyful tidings, hastened herself to the window, and, seeing Aladdin, immediately opened it. The noise of opening the window made Aladdin turn his head that way, and perceiving the princess, he saluted her with an air that expressed his joy. "To lose no time," said she to him, "I have sent to have the private door opened for you; enter and come up."

The private door, which was just under the princess's apartment, was soon opened, and Aladdin conducted up into the chamber. It is impossible to express the joy of both at seeing each other after so cruel a separation. After embracing and shedding tears of joy, they sat down, and Aladdin said: "I beg of you, princess, to tell me what is become of an old lamp which stood upon a shelf in my robing-chamber."

"Alas!" answered the princess, "I was afraid our misfortune might be owing to that lamp; and what grieves me most is, that I have been the cause of it. I was foolish enough to change the old lamp for a new one, and the next morning I found myself in this unknown country, which I am told is Africa."

"Princess," said Aladdin, interrupting her, "you have explained all by telling me we are in Africa. I desire you only to tell me if you know where the old lamp now is." "The African magician carries it carefully wrapt up in his bosom," said the princess; "and this I can assure you, because he pulled it out before me, and showed it to me in triumph."

"Princess," said Aladdin, "I think I have found the means to deliver you and to regain possession of the lamp on which all my prosperity depends; to execute this design it is necessary for me to go to the town. I shall return by noon, and will then tell you what must be done by you to insure success. In the meantime, I shall disguise myself, and beg that the private door may be opened at the first knock."

When Aladdin was out of the palace, he looked round him on all sides, and perceiving a peasant going into the country, hastened after him, and when he had overtaken him, made a proposal to him to change clothes, which the man agreed to. When they had made the exchange, the countryman went about his business, and Aladdin entered the neighbouring city. After traversing several streets, he came to that part of the town where the merchants and artisans had their particular streets according to their trades. He went into that of the druggists; and entering one of the largest and best-furnished shops, asked the druggist if he had a certain powder, which he named.

The druggist, judging Aladdin by his habit to be very poor, told him he had it, but that it was very dear; upon which Aladdin, penetrating his thoughts, pulled out his purse and, showing him some gold, asked for half a dram of the powder; which the druggist weighed and gave him, telling him the price was a piece of gold. Aladdin put the money into his hand, and hastened to the palace, which he entered at once by the private door. When he came into the princess's apartments, he said to her: "Princess, you must take your part in the scheme which I propose for our deliverance. You must overcome your aversion to the magician and assume a most friendly manner toward him, and ask him to oblige you by partaking of an entertainment in your apartments. Before he leaves, ask him to exchange cups with you, which he, gratified at the honour you do him, will gladly do, when you must give him the cup containing this powder. On drinking it, he will instantly fall asleep, and we will obtain the lamp, whose slaves will do our bidding and restore us and the palace to the capital of China."

The princess obeyed to the utmost her husband's instructions. She assumed a look of pleasure on the next visit of the magician, and asked him to an entertainment, which he most willingly accepted. At the close of the evening, during which the princess had tried all she could to please him, she asked him to exchange cups with her and, giving the signal, had the drugged cup brought to her, which she gave to the magician. He drank it out of compliment to the princess, to the very last drop, when he fell backward lifeless on the sofa.

The princess, in anticipation of the success of her scheme, had so placed her women from the great hall to the foot of the staircase, that the word was no sooner given that the African magician was fallen backward, than the door was opened and Aladdin admitted to the hall. The princess rose from her seat, and ran, overjoyed, to embrace him; but he stopped her, and said: "Princess, retire to your apartment; and let me be left alone, while I endeavour to transport you back to China as speedily as you were brought from thence."

When the princess, her women, and slaves were gone out of the hall, Aladdin shut the door, and going directly to the dead body of the magician, opened his vest, took out the lamp which was carefully wrapped up, and rubbing it, the genie immediately appeared. "Genie," said Aladdin, "I command thee to transport this palace instantly to the place from whence it was brought hither." The genie bowed his head in token of obedience and disappeared. Immediately the palace was transported into China, and its removal was felt only by two little shocks, the one when it was lifted up, the other when it was set down, and both in a very short interval of time.

On the morning after the restoration of Aladdin's palace, the sultan was looking out of his window and mourning over the fate of his daughter, when he thought that he saw the vacancy created by the disappearance of the palace to be again filled up.

On looking more attentively, he was convinced beyond

the power of doubt that it was his son-in-law's palace. Joy and gladness succeeded to sorrow and grief. He at once ordered a horse to be saddled, which he mounted that instant, thinking he could not make haste enough to the place.

Aladdin rose that morning by daybreak, put on one of the most magnificent habits his wardrobe afforded, and went up into the hall of twenty-four windows, from whence he perceived the sultan approaching, and received him at the foot of the great staircase, helping him to dismount.

He led the sultan into the princess's apartment. The happy father embraced her with tears of joy; and the princess, on her side, afforded similar testimonies of her extreme pleasure. After a short interval devoted to mutual explanations of all that had happened, the sultan restored Aladdin to his favour, and expressed his regret for the apparent harshness with which he had treated him. "My son," said he, "be not displeased at my proceedings against you; they arose from my paternal love, and therefore you ought to forgive the excesses to which it hurried me." "Sire," replied Aladdin, "I have not the least reason to complain of your conduct, since you did nothing but what your duty required. This infamous magician, the basest of men, was the sole cause of my misfortune."

The African magician, who was thus twice foiled in

his endeavour to ruin Aladdin, had a younger brother who was as skilful a magician as himself, and exceeded him in hatred and wickedness of mankind. By mutual agreement they communicated with each other once a year, however widely separated might be their place of residence from each other. The younger brother, not having received as usual his annual communication, prepared to take a horoscope and ascertain his brother's proceedings. He, as well as his brother, always carried a geomantic square instrument about him; he prepared the sand, cast the points, and drew the figures. On examining the planetary crystal, he found that his brother was no longer living, but had been poisoned; and by another observation, that he was in the capital of the kingdom of China; also that the person who had poisoned him was of mean birth, though married to a princess, a sultan's daughter.

When the magician had informed himself of his brother's fate, he resolved immediately to avenge his death, and at once departed for China; where, after crossing plains, rivers, mountains, deserts, and a long tract of country without delay, he arrived after incredible fatigues. When he came to the capital of China, he took lodging at a khan. His magic art soon revealed to him that Aladdin was the person who had been the cause of the death of his brother. He had heard, too, all the persons of repute in the city talking of a woman called Fatima, who was retired from the world, and of the miracles she wrought. As he fancied that this woman might be serviceable to him in the project he had conceived, he made more minute inquiries, and requested to be informed more particularly who that holy woman was, and what sort of miracles she performed.

"What!" said the person whom he addressed, "have you never seen or heard of her? She is the admiration of the whole town, for her fasting, her austerities, and her exemplary life. Except Mondays and Fridays, she never stirs out of her little cell, and on those days on which she comes into the town she does an infinite deal of good; for there is not a person who is diseased but she puts her hand on them and cures them."

Having ascertained the place where the hermitage of this holy woman was, the magician went at night and, plunging a poniard into her heart, killed this good woman. In the morning he dyed his face of the same hue as hers, and arraying himself in her garb, taking her veil, the large necklace she wore round her waist, and her stick, went straight to the palace of Aladdin.

As soon as the people saw the holy woman, as they imagined him to be, they presently gathered about him in a great crowd. Some begged blessings, others kissed his hand, and others, more reserved, only the hem of his garment; while others, suffering from disease, stooped for him to lay his hands upon them; which he did, muttering some words in form of prayer, and, in short, counterfeiting so well, that everybody took him for the holy woman. He came at last to the square before Aladdin's palace. The crowd and the noise were so great that the princess, who was in the hall of four-and-twenty windows, heard it and asked what was the matter. One of her women told her it was a great crowd of people collected about the holy woman, to be cured of diseases by the imposition of her hands.

The princess, who had long heard of this holy woman but had never seen her, was very desirous to have some conversation with her; which the chief officer perceiving, told her it was an easy matter to bring her to her, if she desired and commanded it, and the princess expressing her wishes, he immediately sent four slaves for the pretended holy woman.

As soon as the crowd saw the attendants from the palace, they made way; and the magician, perceiving also that they were coming for him, advanced to meet them, overjoyed to find his plot succeed so well. "Holy woman," said one of the slaves, "the princess wants to see you, and has sent us for you." "The princess does me too great an honour," replied the false Fatima; "I am ready to obey her command," and at the same time followed the slaves to the palace.

When the pretended Fatima had made her obeisance, the princess said: "My good mother, I have one thing to request, which you must not refuse me; it is, to stay with me, that you may edify me with your way of living, and that I may learn from your good example." "Princess," said the counterfeit Fatima, "I beg of you not to ask what I cannot consent to without neglecting my prayers and devotion." "That shall be no hindrance to you," answered the princess; "I have a great many apartments unoccupied; you shall choose which you like best, and have as much liberty to perform your devotions as if you were in your own cell."

The magician, who really desired nothing more than to introduce himself into the palace, where it would be a much easier matter for him to execute his designs, did not long excuse himself from accepting the obliging offer which the princess made him. "Princess," said he, "whatever resolution a poor wretched woman as I am may have made to renounce the pomp and grandeur of this world, I dare not presume to oppose the will and commands of so pious and charitable a princess."

Upon this the princess, rising up, said: "Come with me, I will show you what vacant apartments I have, that you may make choice of that you like best." The magician followed the princess, and of all the apartments she showed him, made choice of that which was the worst, saying that it was too good for him, and that he accepted it only to please her.

Afterward the princess would have brought him back

into the great hall to make him dine with her; but he, considering that he should then be obliged to show his face, which he had always taken care to conceal with Fatima's veil, and fearing that the princess should find out that he was not Fatima, begged of her earnestly to excuse him, telling her that he never ate anything but bread and dried fruits, and desiring to eat that slight repast in his own apartment. The princess granted his request, saying: "You may be as free here, good mother, as if you were in your own cell; I will order you a dinner, but remember I expect you as soon as you have finished your repast."

After the princess had dined, and the false Fatima had been sent for by one of the attendants, he again waited upon her. "My good mother," said the princess, "I am overjoyed to see so holy a woman as yourself, who will confer a blessing upon this palace. But now I am speaking of the palace, pray how do you like it? And before I show it all to you, tell me first what you think of this hall."

Upon this question, the counterfeit Fatima surveyed the hall from one end to the other. When he had examined it well, he said to the princess: "As far as such a solitary being as I am, who am unacquainted with what the world calls beautiful, can judge, this hall is truly admirable; there wants but one thing." "What is that, good mother?" demanded the princess; "tell me, I adjure you. For my part, I always believed, and have heard say, it wanted nothing; but if it does, it shall be supplied."

"Princess," said the false Fatima, with great dissimulation, "forgive me the liberty I have taken; but my opinion is, if it can be of any importance, that if a roc's egg were hung up in the middle of the dome, this hall would have no parallel in the four quarters of the world, and your palace would be the wonder of the universe."

"My good mother," said the princess, "what is a roc, and where may one get an egg?" "Princess," replied the pretended Fatima, "it is a bird of prodigious size, which inhabits the summit of Mount Caucasus; the architect who built your palace can get you one."

After the princess had thanked the false Fatima for what she believed her good advice, she conversed with her upon other matters; but could not forget the roc's egg, which she resolved to request of Aladdin when next he should visit his apartments. He did so in the course of that evening, and shortly after he entered, the princess thus addressed him: "I always believed that our palace was the most superb, magnificent, and complete in the world; but I will tell you now what it wants, and that is a roc's egg hung up in the midst of the dome." "Princess," replied Aladdin, "it is enough that you think it wants such an ornament; you shall see by the diligence which I use in obtaining it, that there is nothing which I would not do for your sake."

Aladdin left the Princess Buddir al Buddoor that moment, and went up into the hall of four-and-twenty windows, where, pulling out of his bosom the lamp, which after the danger he had been exposed to he always carried about him, he rubbed it; upon which the genie immediately appeared. "Genie," said Aladdin, "I command thee, in the name of this lamp, bring a roc's egg to be hung up in the middle of the dome of the hall of the palace." Aladdin had no sooner pronounced these words, than the hall shook as if ready to fall; and the genie said in a loud and terrible voice: "Is it not enough that I and the other slaves of the lamp have done everything for you, but you, by an unheard-of ingratitude must command me to bring my master, and hang him up in the midst of this dome? This attempt deserves that you, the princess, and the palace, should be immediately reduced to ashes; but you are spared because this request does not come from yourself. Its true author is the brother of the African magician, your enemy whom you have destroyed. He is now in your palace, disguised in the habit of the holy woman Fatima, whom he has murdered; at his suggestion your wife makes this pernicious demand. His design is to kill you, therefore take care of yourself." After these words the genie disappeared.

ALADDIN; OR, THE WONDERFUL LAMP

Aladdin resolved at once what to do. He returned to the princess's apartment and, without mentioning a word of what had happened, sat down and complained of a great pain which had suddenly seized his head. On hearing this, the princess told him how she had invited the holy Fatima to stay with her, and that she was now in the palace; and at the request of the prince, ordered her to be summoned to her at once.

When the pretended Fatima came, Aladdin said: "Come hither, good mother; I am glad to see you here at so fortunate a time. I am tormented with a violent pain in my head, and request your assistance, and hope you will not refuse me that cure which you impart to afflicted persons." So saying, he arose, but held down his head. The counterfeit Fatima advanced toward him, with his hand all the time on a dagger concealed in his girdle under his gown; which Aladdin, observing, he snatched the weapon from his hand, pierced him to the heart with his own dagger, and then pushed him down on the floor.

"My dear prince, what have you done?" cried the princess, in surprise. "You have killed the holy woman!" "No, my princess," answered Aladdin with emotion, "I have not killed Fatima, but a villain who would have assassinated me if I had not prevented him. This wicked man," added he, uncovering his face, "is the brother of the magician who attempted our ruin. He

265

has strangled the true Fatima, and disguised himself in her clothes with intent to murder me." Aladdin then informed her how the genie had told him these facts, and how narrowly she and the palace had escaped destruction through his treacherous suggestion which had led to her request.

Thus was Aladdin delivered from the persecution of the two brothers, who were magicians. Within a few years afterward, the sultan died in a good old age, and as he left no male children, the Princess Buddir al Buddoor succeeded him, and she and Aladdin reigned together many years, and left a numerous and illustrious posterity.

THE END